DEATH AT THE
DEEP DIVE

WE ONLY SEE THE THINGS ON THE SURFACE...

When Pirate Cove's favorite
mystery bookstore owner
and sometimes-amateur sleuth Ellery Page
discovers a vintage diving collection bag
full of antique gold coins
tucked away for safe-keeping
in the stockroom of the Crow's Nest,
it sets off a series of
increasingly dangerous events,
culminating in Jack Carson
trying to cook dinner.
Er...culminating in murder.

DEATH AT THE
DEEP DIVE

SECRETS & SCRABBLE BOOK SEVEN

JOSH LANYON

VELLICHOR BOOKS

An imprint of JustJoshin Publishing, Inc.

DEATH AT THE DEEP DIVE: AN M/M COZY MYSTERY
(Secrets and Scrabble Book 7)
August 2022
Copyright (c) 2021 by Josh Lanyon
Edited by Keren Reed
Cover and book design by Kevin Burton Smith
All rights reserved

Published in the United States of America

JustJoshin Publishing, Inc.
3053 Rancho Vista Blvd.
Suite 116
Palmdale, CA 93551
www.joshlanyon.com

To my dear friend Janet, Happy Birthday, my autumn sister. Shine on forever.

Fifteen men on the dead man's chest–
...Yo-ho-ho, and a bottle of rum!
Drink and the devil had done for the rest–
...Yo-ho-ho, and a bottle of rum!"

–"Dead Man's Chest"
Robert Louis Stevenson

CHAPTER ONE

Eight gold coins gleamed and glinted in the lamplight.

Make that eight gold coins and one silver.

Ellery Page, owner and proprietor of the quaint mystery bookshop known as the Crow's Nest, let out a long breath and picked up the silver coin, fingertips tracing the unfamiliar size and design. It looked old. Very old. On one side a woman held two wreaths aloft. He could just make out the (Latin?) words SÆCVLA VINCIT and below: VIRTVTI ET HONORI. The other side was etched (engraved?) with the profile of a young man and the words PHILIPPUS D.G. HISPAN INFANS

So…Spanish?

Was the image supposed to be King Philip?

He had no idea. He wasn't even sure if the coins were real.

Granted, they *looked* real. The details of the gold pieces—the believably worn engravings, the rough, slightly misshapen edges, even the heft of the coins—doubloons?—felt real.

Seemed legit.

Appearances could be deceptive. But if this was indeed Vernon Shandy's diving collection bag—and whose else could it be?—was it likely the coins would be fake?

Granted, when it came to the Shandy clan, some kind of elaborate scam was always a possibility, but given Vernon's untimely and mysterious disappearance in the 1960s...

Eyes still on the small pile of coins, Ellery reached for his cell phone and pressed the contact number for Pirate Cove's chief of police Jack Carson.

Jack's phone rang once, and then Jack, who also happened to be Ellery's boyfriend, said, "Hey, I'm not quite done here. Did you want to go ahead and grab a table?"

"Uh...do you think you could maybe stop by here for a couple of minutes?"

Jack's tone changed. "You okay? What's up?"

"I'm okay, but...I'd rather not say any more until you get here."

"Are you being held hostage?"

Jack was kidding, of course, though given Buck Island's—and Ellery's—history, maybe anything seemed possible to him.

"No. I'm alone. I...found something."

Jack said crisply, "On my way," and disconnected.

Poor Jack. He thinks I found another body.

Ellery started to put his phone down, but stopped. If these coins *were* the real thing, how valuable were they?

A quick search of Wikipedia elicited the following information:

The doubloon (from Spanish doblón, or "double", i.e. double escudo) was a two-escudo gold coin worth approximately $4 (four Spanish dollars) or 32 reales, and weighing 6.766 grams (0.218 troy ounce) of 22-karat gold (or 0.917 fine; hence 6.2 g fine gold).

Translation, please?

More searching unearthed a 1989 *Los Angeles Times* article and the news that early pieces of eight were hand-made and known as cobs. Higher quality versions were machine-made. And Spanish milled dollars were worth about $50 to $350.

So, if a gold doubloon was worth $350 in 1989, presumably it was worth more now?

As a last resort, Ellery tried eBay. As he scanned the listings for gold coins dated circa 1700s (just on the off-chance that these really had come from the legendary wreck of the pirate galleon known as the *Blood Red Rose*), he sucked in his breath and let it out in a sound typically only heard from maiden aunts when their prize Pekingese tried to, er, get jiggy with a stray.

US $32,500.00

US $39,500.00

US $46,500.00

US $75,000.00

US $124,500.00

"*Yikes.*"

Watson, Ellery's black-spaniel-mix puppy, stopped gnawing his chew toy to gaze in startled inquiry.

Granted, the coins listed for sale were in mint condition with certificates to prove their provenance, but this answered one question: yes, the items in the collection bag were valuable. In fact, that small mound of metal on his desk probably qualified as treasure.

Pirate's treasure.

Eight gold coins worth—just taking the low-end figure—two hundred and sixty thousand dollars? People committed murder for less.

Ellery glanced instinctively at the ceiling entrance to the bookshop attic. Little more than a month ago, someone—

and he had a pretty good idea who—had broken into the Crow's Nest, likely searching for this very collection bag.

Alarm coiled down his spine. Never mind the attic. Had he locked the front door? He couldn't remember.

Ellery rose, left his office, striding past the sales desk, the large oil paintings of pirate galleons battling stormy seas and changing tides, hopping over Watson, who thought this was a terrific new game, down the aisles of towering bookshelves. He reached the front entrance and moved to slide the lock. At the same moment the brass bell chimed as someone started to open the door.

Ellery exclaimed in alarm and slammed shut the door.

On the other side of the divided glass panes, an exasperated Jack called, "You called *me*, remember?"

Ellery yanked the door open. "Sorry."

"What's going on?" Jack ignored Watson who, wishing to claim his share of the welcome, was jumping up and down. "Why are you so spooked?"

"I— It might be easier if I show you."

Jack's dark eyebrows shot up. He said cautiously, "Are you going to show me something living or something...no longer living?"

Ellery laughed shakily. "I'm going to show you an inanimate object."

"Thank God for that. One more body and people will start to talk."

Ellery, headed back toward his office, threw over his shoulder, "I'm pretty sure they're already talking."

Jack, stopping to pat Watson, replied, "I'm pretty sure you're right." He straightened, followed Ellery into his office, stopping short in the doorway. He took a moment to study the litter of water-stained diving bag and coins. "I thought the collection bag was stolen when the bookshop was broken into."

"I did too. But I decided to finally reorganize the storage closet, and when I started pulling stuff out, I found the bag in the very back."

"How is that possible?"

Ellery shook his head. "But this explains why Tackle Shandy—or whoever it was— thought it was worth the risk."

"I'd say so." Jack sounded grim. "If these coins are genuine, they must be worth a fortune."

"I did a little comparison shopping on eBay while I was waiting for you to arrive, and this haul could be worth anything from a quarter of a million to more than a million. Depending on where and when the coins were minted."

Jack's blue-green gaze held Ellery's. "A million dollars?"

Ellery nodded.

"That's a lot of clams."

"If they're genuine."

"Yeah. Okay, well, first things first. This haul is going straight into the evidence locker down at the station. Tomorrow I'll phone the Rhode Island Marine Archaeology Project in Newport."

"I'm just going to grab some quick pics." Ellery held his phone up.

Jack nodded absently. He was studying the ceiling entrance to the attic. He did not look happy.

Ellery moved around the desk, snapping photos of each coin, front and back. He wasn't sure why, exactly. Once the coins were in the hands of RIMAP, they were no longer his problem. He might never even see them again, outside of a museum—ideally, a Buck Island museum.

He paused to examine one coin, then held it out to Jack. "Can you tell what that says? The tiny writing to the left of HISP? Is that a date?"

Jack held the coin beneath the lamp, squinting at the worn engraving. "Maybe 1611?"

"Could that be right?"

"1611? Yes. If these are the real thing, well, the 1650s to 1730s were the golden age of piracy."

"You know what this means?" Ellery glanced at Jack, who looked resigned.

"What do you think it means?"

"Everyone seems to think that diving suit we found in Buccaneer's Bay originally belonged to Vernon Shandy."

"And the collection bag was part of the suit."

"Right. And Tackle himself said Vernon was obsessed with finding the *Blood Red Rose*. That he spent all his spare time hunting for her."

Jack smiled. "You think these coins are from the *Blood Red Rose*. You think Vernon found Captain Blood's ship."

"Yes. I do."

"But don't you think, if Vernon found the *Blood Red Rose*, he'd have told someone?"

Ellery considered. "Yeah. He would. He'd have to. He couldn't retrieve her treasure on his own. He'd probably share that information with certain family members. I don't know that he'd share it with everyone, and no way with anyone outside the Shandy family circle."

Jack grunted. The Shandys were one of Buck Island's oldest and most notorious families. They kept themselves to their selves, and their relationship with law enforcement was wary at best.

Wary on both sides, truth be told.

Jack said, "If the coins are real—and they look real, I agree, but neither of us are experts—then you could be right."

"And if we're right about that," Ellery said, "then you know what else I think?"

Jack studied him for a thoughtful moment. He sighed. "You think Vernon Shandy was murdered."

"I sure do," Ellery replied.

CHAPTER TWO

"**W**hat'll you have to drink, gents?" Though the pub was nearly empty, Tom Tulley appeared to be in a jovial mood when Ellery and Jack sat down at their usual table at the Salty Dog.

By October, the tourists were mostly gone and the island returned to its (in the view of the citizens of Pirate's Cove) rightful owners. The days were cool and crisp, luminous with autumn's gorgeous, golden light. The ocean was still warm enough for swimming, and it was easy to get a good table in any restaurant or bar without a wait. The chilly nights were fragrant with the scent of woodsmoke and damp earth. Twilight strolls along the beach were lit by meteor showers and the white, silky filaments of milkweed pods.

"What was that blue cocktail you made for me last Friday?" Ellery shrugged out of his jacket with Jack's help. Jack had the unobtrusive, courtly gesture thing down to a science. He moved away to hang their jackets on the hooks near the door.

"Blueberry iceberg," Tom answered. "Libby came up with that recipe. Blueberry vodka, Blue Curaçao, lime juice, and a splash of sparkling water."

"That was great. I'll have that again."

Tom nodded, asked Jack, "How about you, Chief? The usual?"

Jack's *usual* was whatever was on tap. He nodded. "How's Libby doing?"

Tom's daughter, Libby, was away at college on the mainland.

"Thriving," Tom said gloomily. Libby was the light of his life, and he missed her dearly.

Ellery, studying the new addition of a blackboard menu, inquired, "What's the End of Summer Special?"

"Secret family recipe."

Jack and Ellery exchanged looks. Jack said, "What do you want to bet Fritos are involved?"

Tom looked outraged. "Hey, how dare you reveal my secrets!" He grinned broadly and departed with their drink order.

"He's in a good mood," Ellery remarked.

"It's October. Everyone cheers up once the tourists leave."

Which seemed counterintuitive for a community that pretty much subsisted on the tourist trade, but even with only one summer under his belt, Ellery got it. Buck Island during tourist season was a different planet from Buck Island the rest of the year.

He and Jack chatted about the ongoing renovations at Captain's Seat, the ramshackle Victorian mansion Ellery had inherited from his great-great-great-aunt Eudora. The previous month, Ellery had finally received a nice chunk of change from Brandon Abbott's estate, allowing him to move ahead with crucial if unglamorous things like electrical repairs and replacing the roof.

Tom returned with their drinks. They both ordered the fish and chips, to Tom's disappointment, and then, as he once more departed, clinked their glasses.

"Cheers," Jack said.

"Yo ho ho," Ellery replied. He sipped his cobalt cocktail. "*Mm.*" The tart sweetness of the cocktail and the crackling warmth of the nearby fireplace were the perfect pairing for a chilly autumn night. He felt like he'd been waiting to exhale ever since dumping those coins on his desk. "I have to say I'm very relieved you-know-what is you-know-where. The thought that it was just lying there in that cupboard all this time makes me feel a little queasy."

"Any chance that it wasn't in the cupboard the whole time? I thought Felix said he left it out on a storage shelf."

Felix Jones, Libby Tulley's boyfriend and the son of Pirate Cove's previous mayor, had pitched in for a short time at the Crow's Nest while Ellery had been convalescing.

"He must have been mistaken. It was his last day at work and his last day on the island, so it's no wonder if he was distracted. When I asked him, he barely remembered Cap giving him the bag."

Jack made a noncommittal noise and sipped his beer.

"Whoever broke in would have to have been in a hurry."

Jack conceded, "The assumption would be you had looked in the bag and so it was unlikely to have been left in the shop at all."

"Exactly!"

Jack studied Ellery for a moment. His smile twisted. "Let's not get ahead of ourselves. First off, there's no proof the collection bag you found belonged to Vernon Shandy. The assumption is the deep dive suit was his, but there are plenty of other divers on this island. No one knows for a fact who hid that suit in the warehouse with the Historical Society's collection. Or for what reason."

"To hide those coins," Ellery said.

Jack shook his head. "That's an assumption."

"It's a working theory. And it's the most logical."

"Maybe. But let's say you're right. Let's go with your *theory* that the suit belonged to the Shandys and that the suit was stashed away to hide the coins."

"Doubloons."

Jack laughed. "You really do love the idea of pirate's treasure, don't you? If your eyes were any shinier, they'd be glowing."

Ellery laughed and sat back in his chair. He shrugged. "Okay, yes. I do love the idea of pirate's treasure."

"Especially pirate's treasure with a mystery attached."

Ellery couldn't help pointing out, "Wouldn't all pirates' treasures have a certain amount of mystery attached?"

"Hm. Good point. But here's what I was getting at. Even if we go with your theory about who owned the collection bag and why it was concealed, it still doesn't prove those coins came from the *Blood Red Rose*."

"*Ah.* Okay. You're right."

"There are a lot of wrecks in the waters around this island."

"True. I'll give you that one."

Jack laughed. "Thank you. And finally, even if your theories are correct about who owned the diving suit and collection bag, where the coins came from, and why they were hidden in the Historical Society's collection, there's still no proof that Vernon Shandy was murdered."

"I wouldn't go that far," Ellery objected. "*Something* happened to him."

"Something, yes. One way or the other, he left the island. That's for sure. But the surrounding circumstances are unknown." As Ellery opened his mouth to debate this, Jack continued, "And there are plenty of reasons the Shandys might want to conceal those circumstances."

Tom returned to the table, bearing platters of golden deep-fried fish, crispy french fries, and tangy coleslaw. He set the sizzling plates before them. "Another round?"

Jack asked Ellery, "Are you driving back to Captain's Seat or staying over?"

There had been a time, not so long ago, when Jack would not have so casually or so openly asked that question.

Ellery smiled. "If Watson and I haven't worn out our welcome?"

Jack gave him the slightest of winks and said to Tom, "Another round, thanks." He added to Ellery, "We can always walk home."

Tom gave Ellery a droll look. "Coming right up!"

Tom departed, Ellery and Jack reached for the salt and pepper shakers, exchanged the vinegar bottle, repositioned the little jars of tartar sauce.

Jack broke off a piece of fried cod and said, as though there had been no interruption, "I'm not trying to bust your balloon. Obviously, there's an element of mystery surrounding these events. It just doesn't automatically, inevitably indicate murder."

"Well, no, of course not." Ellery chewed thoughtfully on a french fry.

Jack observed him for a moment. "Which isn't going to stop you from poking your nose into other people's business and asking a lot of awkward questions, is it?"

Ellery's brows shot up in surprise. "*Me?* Come on, Jack, whatever happened to Vernon Shandy is none of my business. Anyway, even if something sinister did occur, it was over half a century ago. Nobody's going to remember anything this long after the fact. Assuming anyone involved is still around. Which is unlikely. Right?"

Jack sighed, shook his head. "That's what I thought."

CHAPTER THREE

"**S**o Vernon Shandy *did* find the *Blood Red Rose*!" Nora greeted Ellery when she arrived at the Crow's Nest early Friday morning.

There had been a time when Ellery would have been amazed, even shocked, to discover that Nora Sweeny, assistant manager at the Crow's Nest, already knew about his discovery of the gold doubloons. But in the eight months he'd lived on Buck Island, he'd gained a healthy respect for Pirate Cove's, er, wireless communication system, i.e., local gossip network.

"That's not for sure," Ellery cautioned her. "We won't even know if the coins are genuine until RIMAP has a chance to examine them."

"Pshaw." Nora accepted her vanilla-raspberry latte with a nod of thanks. "You know as well as I do those coins are genuine—and where they came from."

Ellery shook his head, but he tended to agree with Nora. For the sake of argument, he said, "There are at least five major shipwrecks off the coast."

"At the *very* least. And over twenty other shipwrecks, though how a shipwreck could ever be anything but major, I fail to see."

She had a point there. Sir Francis Drake himself had re-ferred to the island as *a veritable stumbling-block in the way of the anxious navigator.*

Nora added, "In any case, dearie, Vernon Shandy was only interested in one particular shipwreck."

"The *Blood Red Rose.*"

"*Exactly.*"

"Unfortunately," Ellery said, "Vernon didn't leave a map marked with a giant *X* rolled up in his diving bag, so I'm not sure there'll be any way to prove where those coins came from, let alone pinpoint the position of the ship."

Nora ignored what she no doubt considered a pusillan-imous response. "To think that bag was in the cupboard since August."

"I know." The realization that possibly a million dollars' worth of gold coins had been casually stuffed in there with out-of-date sales signs and Libby's discarded Little Cat tote bag was truly horrifying.

"Now we'll be flooded with treasure hunters searching for the ship." Like most of the islanders, Nora had a love/hate relationship with mainlanders.

"It's not like we don't already have plenty of treasure hunters diving these waters," Ellery pointed out. "Nor are these coins a recent discovery. If Vernon Shandy did find Captain Blood's ship, it happened nearly sixty years ago. Time and tide."

Time and tide was island-speak for *nothing stays the same.* And what could be more true of oceans—hotbeds of geological activity—or eighteenth century shipwrecks?

Nora retorted, "*I* know that, and *you* know that, but you'll be disheartened to discover we're going to be in the minori-ty. There's something about the idea of pirate's treasure that seems to wash the commonsense out of people's heads." She glumly sipped her latte.

Maybe she had a point, given the idiotic things people did for an opportunity to be on TV. Himself included.

As if the universe was listening in on his thoughts, Ellery's cell phone rang. He glanced at the number and was surprised to see the contact number for his agent, Ronny.

Once, his heart would have pinballed around his chest hitting every light, lever, bumper, and vital organ in his desperate hope for some good news, but now he felt only surprise and a little curiosity. Ronny had rejected the last screenplay Ellery had submitted (in fairness, Ronny would not have considered her request for a rewrite an out-and-out rejection), and Ellery's audition days were behind him.

"I'm just going to step into my office to take this," he told Nora.

Nora nodded absently, her attention on the shop's tall windows and the swift approach of Kingston Peabody, their newest "team member" (as the companies that sold employee motivational gifts would have it).

Ellery clicked to answer his cell, saying, "This is a surprise," as he stepped into his office. He closed the door.

"Prepare yourself for a bigger surprise," Ronny said briskly. "The *Happy Halloween! You're Dead* franchise is getting a reboot."

"Wait. Don't *I* now own the *Happy Halloween! You're Dead* franchise?"

"I was curious about that too," Ronny admitted. "So I did some checking. It seems Brandon signed the deal for the reboot shortly before his death. He got a *major* deal, which is how he could afford to pay cash for the house on Skull Island."

"Uh, it's Skull House on Buck Island."

"Whatever, kiddo. But I wouldn't go anywhere near that place if I were you."

"It's on the other side of— Anyway."

"*Anyway*, it's a done deal. Brandon got the cash, and the reboot is happening. It's a three-movie deal with Black Palace Entertainment."

"Black Palace. Is that Vincent Raimi's studio?"

"Yep. He's got Dick Waller onboard to direct. Dex Zimmerman is drafting the screenplay. And Timon Grantham is SFX."

Ellery said slowly, doubtfully, "That's some serious talent."

"I know. Here's the relevant bit. They want you for the part of Noah Street Junior's father."

It took a second or two for that to sink in. "Noah Street's *father*?"

"Noah Street *Junior's* father." Ronny added quickly, "And I know, you look *fantastic*. You're in your prime. *But* no way can you pass for sixteen now."

"I couldn't pass for sixteen *then*," Ellery protested.

"I don't agree. You were a *very* believable sixteen-year-old. They've signed Fallon Provost to play Noah, and he's twenty-six. You were a baby compared to him."

Fallon Provost? For heaven's sake. These were A-list players. Why in the world would anyone pump so much money into what had been, at best, an obscure B-film franchise?

"I'm thirty-two. How am I supposed to have a sixteen-year-old son?"

"I know we had the birds and bees conversation before. When Lucy Langford tried—"

"That's not what I mean."

"If you'll recall, in Hollywood, there's this thing called *makeup*, and it's really useful for making people look younger—or older—than they are."

"But what happened to John Nealon? Why isn't he playing Noah's father?"

"He's playing Noah *Junior's* grandfather. The studio's idea is that the OG fans will go crazy for all this character continuity, and the new fans will appreciate the meta, because that's how kids are now, but we all know they just want to watch Fallon and Billie shaking sheets."

"Shaking...sheets."

Ellery felt like his head was spinning, which was probably appropriate, though the wrong film franchise. He asked faintly, "Billie who?"

"Billie Watson. You've seen her in everything. She's adorable. You'll love her."

"Yeeeeeah. No. I really don't think so. I mean, I'm retired from acting, Ronny."

Instead of arguing, Ronny began to rattle off numbers like an old-fashioned calculator with a short in the wiring. Ellery would not have been surprised to see cash register paper unfurl from his cell phone. As the numbers sank in, he gulped.

"That makes no sense. I'm—I'd be—supporting cast."

"Honestly? I think they want you all in on this. They're anticipating a huge success, and—"

"*Why?*"

Ronny ignored that. "—since they've only got the rights for three films, they want to be able to come back to you and cut a deal. Also, as you pointed out, you're only thirty-two, you're still hot, and you bring a devoted fan base in a demographic they'd love to capture."

"Come *on*." Ellery was pained at the very thought.

"Also," Ronny said in a careful sort of tone, "it's in the contract they signed with Brandon."

"*What?*"

"Per the contract, you get first right of refusal on the part of Noah Junior's dad."

"If that isn't just like Brandon! He knew how I felt about those films."

"Those films made us *all* a lot of money. And that was without the benefit of an A-list director, writer, and art director. This is not the worst thing that could happen to you."

As much as Ellery wanted to shoot the whole idea down, the figures Ronny had quoted held him silent.

At the same time, he was fully invested in his new life as bookstore owner. He had not only come to terms with the fact that his acting career was over, he was relieved about it.

Still. That money.

But being away from Jack for…who knows how long? A month? Longer? No way.

"I don't want you to think I'm ungrateful, but—"

"Just think about it," Ronny urged. "You don't have to answer right now."

"When does filming begin?"

"Next summer. They haven't locked the production schedule yet."

"I don't want to do it. That's the truth."

Ronny was silent. She had been Ellery's agent for a long time.

Ellery chewed his lip, weighing the pros and cons, thinking about the things he could do with that money. He said at last, reluctantly, "I'll have to think about it. I've got stuff happening now. I've got a-a different life."

"Of course," Ronny said quickly. "I'm sure it's a wonderful life on Skull Island. Take your time. We all want you to make the right decision."

"I don't like feeling that Brandon's still manipulating me."

Ronny considered, said, "Well, I can't speak to that, but maybe it's not quite how you imagine. Brandon didn't know he was going to be murdered, poor guy. Maybe this was his way of reaching out to you. For whatever reason."

From beyond the grave.

Okay, well, maybe a little dramatic. Ronny was right. When Brandon had made that deal, he'd had no idea his days were numbered. And Ellery couldn't complain about the offer Black Palace had made him.

"Maybe. I'll think it over and get back to you within a day or so."

"No rush," Ronny said. "Take your time and think it through. Just remember: offers like this don't come around every day."

Ellery didn't think he'd been on the phone more than a minute or two, but when he opened his office door, he was startled to find a small crowd gathered around the sales desk. Everyone seemed to be talking at once.

Stanley Starling, a regular customer and member of the Silver Sleuths book club, was insisting, "It was 1960. I remember very clearly."

Mr. Starling was a spry, slight man in his seventies. With his tufted hair and habit of popping out startling pronouncements, he reminded Ellery of a geriatric jack-in-the-box.

"I'm fairly sure it was '63, dear," Nora replied.

"It should be easy enough to verify." That was Kingston, a small, dapper man of about seventy. Kingston was by nature a peacemaker.

Hermione Nelson—another member of the Silver Sleuths (Ellery began to get an uneasy feeling about this mini flash mob)—chimed in, "I believe he's correct, dear, because the old mansion on Spring Street burned down in 1960."

With strained patience, Nora replied, "You're perfectly correct, dear. Ballard Hall did burn down in the spring of 1960. However, I'm quite sure we should be looking at the summer of 1963."

Ellery interrupted, "Looking at the summer of 1963 for what?"

Nora, Kingston, Mr. Starling, and Mrs. Nelson all jumped as guiltily as if he'd caught them with their hands in the cash register.

"Oh, we're just discussing the feasibility of putting together a diving exhibit for the Historical Society's new museum." The bright smile Nora offered wouldn't have fooled a baby.

"*Riiiight,*" Ellery said. "And is this diving exhibit going to feature anyone I—"

He broke off as the front door swung open with an impatient jangle of the brass bell.

Déjà vu.

A large and muscular red-haired man dressed in jeans, work boots, and a black T-shirt with a diver's blue silhouette and the immortal words of wisdom *The Deeper You Go The Better It Feels*, gazed at the assembly and rasped, "Ellery Page? My gram wants to see you."

Ellery said cautiously, "Do I know your gram?"

"She knows you. That's the point."

Hm. Was this the demographic Ronny was referring to? Naturally, Ellery kept the thought to himself. Tackle Shandy had a reputation for a number of things, but sense of humor wasn't one of them.

In any case, Watson, perhaps remembering earlier encounters, took instant offense and charged forward.

Arf! Arf! Arf!

Tackle's lip curled. "Somebody better grab that hamster before it gets stepped on."

Kingston and Mr. Starling rushed to rescue Watson, narrowly missing taking each other as they both dived for the pup—and who said Tackle Shandy had no sense of humor? Because he did laugh at that, and his booming *har-har-har* laugh was as cartoony bad-guy as everything else about him. In fact, if it wasn't for that little prison-record thing, Ellery would have dismissed Tackle's schtick as bad acting. (The *other* kind of bad acting. The kind Ellery was familiar with.)

Mr. Starling ended up with the indignantly struggling Watson. He promptly handed the puppy—who was still loudly voicing his opinion of Tackle's manners as well as Mr. Starling's—to Kingston.

"Is there some reason Vera can't use the telephone like normal folk?" Nora asked tartly.

"I guess you'd have to ask her, *Miz* Sweeny," Tackle retorted.

"Never mind, I'm coming." Ellery pointed at Nora. "Mind the store."

Nora spread her arms as though to say, *Need you ask?*

Ellery followed Tackle out the door. The brass bell tolled a final farewell.

CHAPTER FOUR

If someone wanted to get technical, Vera Sutton-Shandy, the elderly matriarch of the Shandy family, was not, in fact, Tackle Shandy's grandmother.

Ellery had trouble following the complicated familial relationships of the islanders in general, and the Shandys' in particular, but according to Nora, Vera was actually Vernon Shandy's sister. Which made her Tackle's...second cousin? Second cousin removed? Something like that. It was moot, because all the Shandys referred to her as Gram.

At a guestimate, the tall, straight, rawboned woman who offered him coffee milk and cigarettes, was probably in her nineties. Her hair was snowy white, her blue eyes had faded to gray, but at one time she would have been striking. In fact, she was still striking, though in more of a don't-cross-the-lady-in-the-leopard-print-leggings sort of way.

He accepted the coffee milk, declined the cigarettes, and seated himself, as directed, next to an old-fashioned birdcage containing a large, elderly parrot. The parrot appeared to be asleep. Or at least, the noise coming from the cage sounded like snoring.

"So you're...Eudora's...nephew," Vera said between puffs of her cigarette.

Great-great-great-nephew, not that Ellery was going to argue the point with a woman everyone called Gram.

"Yep. I'm Ellery."

"How do you like...our...island, Ellery?"

Was there an emphasis on *our* island? He suspected there was.

"I like it. A lot."

Vera cocked a skeptical eyebrow and tipped cigarette ash into a brass clipper ship ashtray. "Think you'll stick around?" She returned to puffing her cigarette. "Or...will you sell out...to some crooked...land developer?"

"I don't plan on selling. To anyone."

She curled her lip, gazing unblinkingly at him and, to avoid what felt like the start of a peculiar staring contest, Ellery glanced around the room.

The house, like its owner, was not at all what he'd expected, but then, what had he expected? A refugee compound built of scrap metal and salvage like something out of *Mad Max*? The reality was a well-groomed aqua-blue Queen Anne Victorian with a white wraparound porch and small private garden in back. An American flag and a black and white MIA flag gallantly furled and unfurled from a small flag pole in the center of the tidy lawn.

The interior was much like the exterior. Antiquated but scrupulously clean and well-cared for. Vera Sutton-Shandy seemed to be a collector of silhouette portraits (or were all those sharp-featured cutouts Shandy ancestors?), porcelain shepherdesses, and—unless he was very much mistaken—scrimshaw.

"You...do have...the Page nose."

Ellery resisted the temptation to touch his nose. What was the proper response? Judging by the appendage prominently displayed in the portrait of his esteemed ancestor, Captain Horatio Page: *Thank you?*

He settled for a neutral, "Ah."

Vera continued to brood and puff. Perhaps he was supposed to get the message through smoke signals?

"They say...you're making a go...of that bookstore."

"I'm trying. Yes."

The parrot suddenly woke up and shrieked, "Ahoy there! Ye scurvy swab!"

"Shut up, Mortimer," Vera said without heat.

"Who loves ya, baby!" returned Mortimer, and tucked his molty head beneath his wing.

Vera ignored Mortimer, abruptly stubbing out her cigarette and directing her steely gray gaze toward Ellery. "I'm not going to beat around the bush. I want you to find out who murdered my brother fifty-nine years ago."

Ellery choked on his coffee milk but managed to recover with barely a splutter.

"That's—I'm not really—*what*?"

"You found the doubloons. You must have heard the story."

"I've heard a lot of stories. You're saying the coins in the collection bag Chief Carson and I found on the *Roussillon* were Vernon's?"

She gave him an impatient look. "Who else's?"

"Well, there've been a lot of divers on this island through the years."

"Most of them don't find gold doubloons."

"I bet a lot of them say they do. Especially now."

Her lip curled again in one of those odd smiles. "You might be right about that. But take my word for it. The coins you found belonged to my brother."

Ellery nodded noncommittally. Little bit of a gray area there. Vera was relying on the Law of Finds—which was the understanding Vernon would have been operating under as well. But in 1987 the US had passed the Abandoned Shipwreck Act, which gave title of all shipwrecks "within US waters" (meaning anything found within three miles off the coastline) to the United States and *not* to the discoverer of the shipwreck. If the legends surrounding the *Blood Red Rose* were true, she had gone down very close to harbor. Obviously, Ellery wasn't going to get into that now.

Vera said, "You found a World War II green canvas bag with a wooden bottom. There are a few holes in the canvas and a wooden, curved rest area and strap to secure a dive tank. One of the leather handles was detached on one end. It might be long gone by now. The handle straps were loose. There was a tag, but the name Virgil Shandy had faded out. The numbers 75-167 were painted on bottom of the bag. The bag itself was about thirty-nine inches long and eighteen inches deep."

Nailed it. With alarming accuracy.

"Okay, I believe you, Mrs. Sutton-Shandy. I believe the bag was your brother's and that he found those coins. But I'm not sure why you're so sure your brother was murdered. I'm also not sure why you think I'd be the best person to find out who killed him."

"I'm not sure you're the best person. But you're probably the person I can most trust."

Ellery smiled, genuinely amused. "How do you figure that?"

"For one thing, you turned a handful of gold doubloons over to Dudley Do-Right. Which was a ninny thing to do. However, it proves you're an honest ninny."

"Gosh, thanks."

Vera's laugh was disconcertingly similar to Tackle's *har-har-har* bellow. "Don't take offense, laddie. You'll soon see

I always speak my mind. Another thing. You didn't oppose young Neddy getting bail."

"Oh, that." Ellery shrugged. The fact of the matter was, he was grateful to Ned, who'd surely had mixed feelings on the subject, for not murdering him when he'd had the chance.

"You have a kind heart. Again, perhaps not the sharpest knife in the drawer, but."

Mortimer the parrot woke up again and screamed, "Ahoy there! Ye scurvy swab!"

"I said shut *up*!" Vera snapped irritably.

"I said shut *up*!" Mortimer returned in the exact tone of voice. And then, coyly, "Who loves ya, baby!"

Ellery preserved a straight face and drank his coffee milk.

"Anyway," Vera continued as though there had been no interruption, "the entire village knows you're a snooper, and since you seem pretty good at it..."

"Well, thank you, I think. But I'm just a private citizen. I don't have the resources the police do—"

"Oh yes, you do." Vera's smile was sly. "There's nothing your pal Jack Carson won't do for you. If you ask him nicely."

"Uh...excuse me?" Ellery's tone was exactly the right shade of how-very-dare-you, but annoyingly, Vera just laughed. Ellery said, "Clearly, we're talking about two different Jack Carsons."

"No doubt we are." She lit another cigarette. "Save your breath, laddie. It's common knowledge."

Ellery spluttered, "It's—*what's* common knowledge? No. I don't care. First of all, no. Wrong. And secondly—*that's* just wrong on every level. But, putting that...that *nonsense* aside, you're talking about *sixty years ago*."

"Fifty-nine."

"That's a cold case. That's a case so cold, it's…"

"Cryogenically frozen?" Vera's expression was one of polite inquiry.

Chalk one up for Vera. Just because she was an elderly woman running a salvage business in a fishing village on a tiny island in the middle of nowhere didn't mean she hadn't ever read a book or watched TV. She was not Pittenweem Jo, for heaven's sake.

Ellery protested, "How do you know your brother was murdered? And if you thought he was murdered, why didn't you go to the police fifty-nine years ago when someone could have actually done something about it?"

"I did go to the police!"

Her unexpected rage—fifty-nine years' worth—startled him into silence.

Vera jumped to her feet as though she couldn't contain herself a minute longer. "You're right! Fifty-nine years ago, I couldn't be sure. I'd only my gut instinct. So I went to the police. But Chief Ballard wouldn't take me seriously. And even if he had, he couldn't find his arse with both hands. I went back a week later, and they treated me like I was some hysterical female. No one would help me. No one believed me. They called him a *deserter*. Vernon!"

"I'm sorry," Ellery said. He knew how it felt to have the police not believe you.

She dropped back into her chair. "I thought Vernon's fate was destined to remain one of the island's mysteries. But then *you* washed up on our shore. The last Page."

"The last…"

"If scuttlebutt is to be believed."

For a moment they simply stared at each other.

He admitted, "The truth is, Mrs. Sutton-Shandy—"

"Never mind that Sutton-Shandy business," she interrupted. "You might as well call me Gram. You've as much right as anyone on this island, and more than some."

"What's that mean?"

She shrugged. "Come now, laddie, you must know the Page and Shandy bloodlines are as intertwined as seaweed in a kelp bed."

Colorful, but surely inaccurate. No way was he calling her *Gram*. Ideally, he wasn't going to call her anything, because he wasn't going to get involved in this very old mur— missing person's case.

But even as the thought formed, he couldn't help thinking that he was passing up the perfect opportunity to find out where those gold doubloons came from.

Oh, who was he kidding? Of *course*, he was curious about what had happened to Vernon Shandy. He'd been curious since he'd first heard Nora mention Shandy's name. Finding the doubloons had only whetted his interest.

He repeated, "The truth is, I wouldn't even know where to begin with a case like this. I'm not a detective. I just get roped into things, usually because I know the people involved. But I don't have any personal connection here. And even if I knew where to start, everyone involved is probably d—" He caught himself. Present company was clearly excepted. He concluded, "Not around to talk to."

Vera studied him for a long moment through the veil of cigarette smoke.

She said finally, "As for where to start, you'd start with me, of course. I've had decades to think about this. I'll provide you with a list of suspects right now." She reached into the little jeweled cigarette box on the table and pulled out a much-handled sheet of lavender paper. She handed the creased sheet across the table to Ellery.

As he unfolded the paper, she added, "Not every suspect is still alive, I'll give you that, but it's not as though I expect you to bring anyone to justice. It's too late, I know. Most of them have found their justice beyond the grave. *But I want to know what happened.* I want the truth! Vernon was my brother, and I loved him dearly. For fifty-nine years, not a day has passed I haven't thought about him, missed him, wondered what happened. It haunts me."

It was pretty effective, not least because she seemed sincere. Her eyes glittered with a brightness that might even have been real tears.

Reluctantly, Ellery stared down at the list.

Joey (Josephine) Franklin

Douglas Franklin

Barry Shandy

Tony Bernard

None of those names meant anything to him. But the last name on the list, *that* was a name he recognized.

Eudora Page

Ellery raised his head and met Vera's bright gaze.

"Eudora Page. My aunt Eudora?"

Vera blew out a stream of blue smoke. "Eudora and Vernon were sweet on each other. I don't suppose anyone told you that."

"No."

"It's the truth. They grew up together, and Eudora, well, no one knew more about this island and its history than Eudora. Especially when it came to our secrets. She could tell you about every ship that went down off this coast. The two of them used to dive together."

"My aunt Eudora used to go *diving* with Vernon Shandy?"

"Why not?"

"Well, but..." Ellery trailed off. Why not indeed? In 1963, Eudora would have been... Actually, he had no idea. He knew virtually nothing about his benefactress.

It seemed Vera read his discomfiture correctly. She burst out with another of those *har-har-har* laughs, waking the parrot, who squawked, "Ahoy there! Ye scurvy swab!"

"Your auntie wasn't born an old woman! She was thirty years old in 1963. Two years younger than Vernon. We were at school together. Hell, yes, she used to dive. When they were kids, she and Vernon spent all their spare time hunting for the *Blood Red Rose*."

It was startling to realize that until that very moment— and despite the fact that he was driving around in her vintage blue VW and living in her decrepit mansion—Ellery had never felt more than an occasional flicker of curiosity about Eudora Page. In fact, this was the first time it had dawned on him that she had not always been an elderly, eccentric hoarder who, for reasons known only to herself, had left all her worldly goods to an unknown, distant nephew instead of a hospital for stray cats.

"Why is she a suspect?"

Vera's expression hardened infinitesimally. "Things were different between them after he joined the Navy. She changed. Vernon changed too. He was colder. Not mean, but not... He was always restless. He started drinking more. And there were other women. Women could never resist him." Her smile was odd. "I don't know if that change was the Navy or Eudora. He went to fight a war Eudora didn't approve of."

Ellery nodded, but the truth was, he didn't know what to make of that. With every new piece of information, Eudora became more real—and more of a stranger.

"Okay, they grew apart. So, again, why would *she* have been a suspect?"

"She had as much motive as anyone. More, given that that treasure probably should have been half hers."

Full circle. Back to the gold doubloons and the lost treasure of the *Blood Red Rose*. It was like working with a broken compass.

"Did Vernon *tell* you he'd found the *Blood Red Rose*?"

She hesitated. "No."

"No. So there's no proof there was ever more than a handful of doubloons. Let alone that there was a motive for my aunt to have murdered her old friend. Why would she? How would that get her the treasure? For God's sake. There's no way."

"You never met her. How do you know?"

"I just know."

Vera shrugged. "Then prove her innocent. *Someone* killed him. That I know. Vernon didn't desert. He didn't fall into a well. He didn't jump off a cliff."

"Maybe someone did kill him, but it wasn't my aunt Eudora."

"That's an awful lot of faith in a woman you never met. Especially when, as far as I could ever discover, Eudora was the last person to see Vernon alive."

Ellery opened his mouth, but Mortimer the parrot shrieked again, "Ahoy there! Ye scurvy swab!"

"Go to sleep!" Vera shouted, then turned to Ellery and said quite calmly, "Would you like to reconsider?"

"Pieces of eight! Pieces of eight!" Mortimer jeered. "Who loves ya, baby!"

CHAPTER FIVE

"**L**ucy, you've got some 'splaining to do," Ellery called when he arrived back at the Crow's Nest.

It was shortly after one when Tackle dropped him off at the bookstore. As Vera's house was no more than a five-minute walk from the harbor, Ellery had been hoping to avoid another of those awkward, silent golf-cart rides with Tackle, but nope. Vera had insisted Tackle would drive him.

And, in fact, though still awkward, this ride had not been silent. No sooner was Vera's house out of sight than Tackle asked, "What made you finally decide to hand that gold over to the authorities?"

"I didn't *finally* decide anything. I only found the collection bag last night."

Tackle's expression was one of open disbelief. "Sure."

Like he cared what some lout with hair growing out of all the wrong places thought? Ellery ignored Tackle.

"Where was it, then?" Tackle persisted, nearly steering them off the road in his effort to keep Ellery under observation.

Ellery met Tackle's blank stare. "Way in the back of the cupboard with all the office supplies."

Tackle continued to stare, then gave a single, short laugh.

And that's what their entire conversation consisted of—both to and from Vera's.

Anyway, he arrived safely and found Kingston washing the large windows facing the harbor. He turned to say, "Nora took the box of donated books to the med center library."

"She didn't have to. I was going to take care of that," Ellery said guiltily. He knelt to pet Watson, who seemed under the impression they had been separated for many a year, wriggling and squirming in delight as Ellery tickled his silky black tummy.

Kingston smiled faintly, watching them. "I believe she wanted to visit Elijah Murphy. He's recovering from back surgery."

"Oh, that's right." Ellery gave Watson a final pat and rose. "Did the Silver Sleuths reach consensus as to who killed Vernon Shandy?"

Kingston chuckled. "I'm afraid not. They were still debating the date of his disappearance when the meeting broke up."

"According to Vera, it was fifty-nine years ago, so Nora was right about it being 1963."

Dirty water rained down as Kingston clamped his squeegee. "In 1963 the Vietnam War was beginning to escalate."

"That was my thought too," Ellery agreed. "But according to Vera, there's zero chance Vernon deserted. Even Nora said Vernon Shandy had no problem going to war and would never have willingly left the island. Not for good."

"She's probably right." Kingston beamed at Ellery. "I envy you the opportunity to speak with Vera. I tried to interview her for the revised edition of *Ghosts of Buck Island*. I'm sure she could tell a tale or two, all those family stories passed down from one generation to the next, but she declined my requests."

"I suspect the Shandys prefer to keep a low profile."

"I suspect you're right. But, oh my word, there are some wonderful legends featuring the Shandys!"

Ellery grinned. "I know. I read the book."

It had started to rain when Nora arrived back at the bookshop about an hour later.

Watson, having had no luck distracting Ellery from bookkeeping or Kingston from window washing (it had been a mistake to start with the outside), scrambled up, snatched the nearest toy, and dropped it temptingly on the toe of Nora's sensible shoe. He wagged his tail hopefully.

Nora shook her head, picked up the blue rubber doughnut, and pitched it with impressive accuracy through the doorway to Ellery's office.

Watson trotted jauntily after.

"You're barking up the wrong tree there, buddy," Ellery told him. And to Nora, "How's Cap Murphy?"

"He'll live," Nora said dismissingly. "A man his age should know better than to climb onto the roof to clean rain gutters. What did Vera have to say for herself? Has she hired you to find out what happened to Vernon?"

"I wouldn't say I've been hired. There was no mention of payment. It was more the suggestion that it might be in all of our best interests if I figured out what actually happened."

"That sounds a little sinister," Kingston remarked.

Nora said, "Not at all. I think it was very sensible of her."

"You don't consider the timing suspicious?"

"Do you?" Nora looked in surprise from Kingston to Ellery.

"I'm not sure," Ellery said. "Vera says her brother's disappearance has haunted her for decades. So maybe the discovery of the coins just brought it all to a head."

Kingston said, "Or maybe, the discovery of the coins served as a warning that the jig was up."

Nora looked intrigued. "Then you believe Vera could be complicit in her brother's disappearance?"

Kingston replied, "Don't you?"

They beamed at each other.

Ellery said, "She's on my list of suspects, for sure."

"Do you *have* a list of suspects?" Nora looked both surprised and pleased at this sign of initiative on Ellery's part.

"Vera gave me her list. Which is one reason she's on mine." He pulled out his phone and showed them the photo he'd snapped of Vera's list.

For a moment or two Nora peered at the list. "Eudora!" She glanced at Ellery in surprise.

"I know."

"Good heavens," Kingston murmured. "If she needed to grab your attention, that would be the way."

Nora's expression grew thoughtful. "Hmm. Yes, I suppose in the interests of complete impartiality, we have to consider Eudora."

"Since when have we ever been concerned with complete impartiality?" Ellery asked. "And why did you never bother to mention I'm apparently, somehow, related to the notorious Shandys?"

"Pshaw. Leave it to Vera to try and claim a family connection." Nora patted his shoulder. "Don't pay any attention to that nonsense. If you go far enough back, we're all related on this island."

Ellery happened to catch Kingston's fleeting expression, and he couldn't help thinking Nora was maybe not being her usual forthcoming self.

She continued to frown over the list on Ellery's screen.

He asked, "Are any of these people still alive?"

"I'm not sure. Barry Shandy is long gone. He was Vernon's Uncle. They shared an obsession for treasure hunting, but they weren't close. In fact, the opposite."

"How long after Vernon's disappearance did Barry die?"

"A few years after. But of course, if we're considering Barry, we'd have to at least look at Rocky. Although a look is about all we can do."

"Who's Rocky?"

"Rocky is Barry's son. He married Ginny Murphy."

"Any relation to Cap Murphy?"

"Yes. Now, Ginny passed in...hmm...2000, was it? Yes, that's right. Because everyone was worried about Y2K and the Millennium Bug."

For a moment, Ellery thought the Millennium Bug was a virus contracted by Ginny, but then he recalled it had to do with everyone fearing the entire computer systems of the world would go haywire when the clocks clicked 00 on January 1.

"Is Rocky still with us?"

"Yes. Rocky lives just a few houses down from Vera. Unfortunately, there are owls in the attic."

"Huh?"

"Rocky's..." She tapped her temple with her index finger.

"Forgetful?"

"Let's say, interviewing him might prove an exercise in frustration."

"Interviewing *everyone* proves an exercise in frustration," Ellery informed her. "Everybody lies. Everybody withholds information. Everyone gets times and dates wrong."

"Witness testimony is extremely unreliable. It's up to the detective to sort the wheat from the chaff."

Ellery restrained himself. "Did Rocky and Ginny have any kids?"

"Oh yes. One." Nora's eyes gleamed. "Tackle Shandy."

Ellery straightened, staring at her. "The same Tackle Shandy who broke in here searching for that collection bag? And broke into Captain's Seat and ransacked the place?"

"Another point to consider. Rocky now lives with Tackle and his wife, June." Nora looked thoughtful. "I wonder why Vera doesn't consider Rocky a suspect?"

Kingston interjected, "Correct me if I'm wrong, but we don't actually have proof it was Tackle who got in through the attic, do we?"

Nora waved this off. "We know it was Tackle."

"It was Tackle," Ellery agreed. "I mean, we can't prove it in a court of law, but I know it was Tackle. He practically admitted it to me back when he was working for Odette Wallace. Did Rocky and Ginny have any other kids?"

"No," Nora said.

"So we can add Tackle to our list."

Kingston cleared his throat. Ellery glanced at him. "No. You're right. Tackle is too young to have had anything to do with Vernon's disappearance. And we have no idea of how many people knew what was in that collection bag. We don't even know for sure the collection bag belonged to Vernon."

"Come now," Nora said. "Did Vera say the collection bag belonged to Vernon?"

"Well, yes."

"Then the bag belonged to Vernon."

"Are you saying Vera wouldn't lie?"

"No," Nora conceded. "Vera would lie her head off if it suited her purposes."

"According to Vera, the bag originally belonged to Virgil Shandy. Which means Kingston's right. There's a possibility another member of the Shandy family was using the bag."

"Virgil Shandy was Vera and Vernon's father. He died in, I believe, 1957. I think we can assume that bag belonged to Vernon. Or, *possibly*, Vera."

Ellery said, "Vera stays on my list of suspects."

"Although...if Vera's our culprit, it seems unlikely she'd initiate an investigation into a crime she committed." Kingston's tone was regretful.

"Maybe it's as you suggested. Now that the doubloons have come to light, she knows an investigation into Vernon's disappearance is inevitable."

Was it inevitable, though? Jack hadn't seemed overly interested in the possibility that Vernon Shandy had met with foul play. Granted, Jack had enough real-time crimes and misdoings to keep him busy.

Kingston said, "Perhaps you're right. It won't hurt to keep Vera on our list of suspects."

Nora ignored them both, staring thoughtfully into space. "I wonder if Joey Franklin was that woman Vernon got involved with after he joined the Navy? The one who used to work at the Deep Dive."

Neither Ellery nor Kingston had anything to offer. They watched Nora as though waiting for the oracle to pronounce.

Nora returned to muttering over the list of Vera's suspects. "Douglas Franklin. What's the connection? Did Vera say?"

"She didn't seem to know anything about him, other than he was married to Josephine and they both worked at the Deep Dive. He was one of the bartenders. She was a waitress. Vera wasn't sure if either of them were still alive or where they might be living."

"The lady, I regret to say, was a tramp. If she's the one I'm thinking of. They had a lot of waitresses over the years. I don't remember the gentleman." Nora frowned, reading the next name on the list. "Tony Bernard. I vaguely recall… He must have been Vernon's Navy buddy. Tall. Very handsome. Of course, they were all *so* handsome in their uniforms."

Ellery and Kingston glanced at each other.

"They went diving a few times. I don't remember if he was here that summer, but if he's on Vera's list, I suppose he must have been."

"How old were you in 1963?" Ellery asked curiously.

Nora raised her brows.

"Sorry. A gentleman doesn't ask?"

"I wouldn't have minded you asking in '63," Nora said. "I was fourteen."

"*Fourteen?*"

"An unusually observant child, I don't doubt," Kingston put in, and Nora's cheeks pinked.

"Sure," Ellery said. It was likely true; Nora probably *had* been an unusually observant child. But she'd still only been fourteen. He had to assume at that age, she'd have missed a lot or misinterpreted some of what she witnessed. Assuming she witnessed much of anything.

"What about Stanley and Hermione?" Kingston inquired.

"Stanley is a year older than me," Nora said. "Hermione couldn't have been more than nine or ten."

"Then I suppose we can rule the three of you out as suspects."

Kingston chuckled. Nora said absently, "In this instance, yes."

"Uh…" But honestly, maybe better to let that go. One mystery at a time.

Finally, Nora handed him back his phone. "Where will you start?" she asked.

Her expression was as innocent as a baby's, but Ellery didn't buy that for a second.

He sighed. "I can't believe what I'm about to say, but given that this investigation requires in-depth knowledge of the island and its history, and you, Mr. Starling, and Mrs. Nelson are about the only three possible witnesses I can trust, I think this might be…"

He didn't *have* to say it. Nora clapped her hands together and exclaimed, "*Yes!* Another case for the Silver Sleuths book club!"

CHAPTER SIX

"**T**ell me you're kidding," Jack said.

"Well, no. But if you think about it—"

"If I think about it, my head's going to explode." But truthfully, Jack sounded resigned, not upset, and Ellery relaxed.

The Crow's Nest was closed for the day. Ellery sat in his office, feet propped comfortably on his desk. He was talking to Jack on the phone, while playing Scrabble GO and listening to the rain wind down and Watson gnaw his bully stick with the ferocity of a tiny wolf having brought down its first stag. Better a stag than another piece of antique furniture at Captain's Seat.

"It's not like I could really keep them out. I mean, if *you* can't scare them straight, how am *I* supposed to do it? They were bound to get involved sooner or later. This way maybe it's more of a controlled burn rather than an actual wildfire."

"Keep telling yourself that, Barbecue."

Ellery had to smile at the idea of a youthful Jack reading G.I. Joe comic books. "At least this time around it's just a puzzle and not an actual…case."

"How do you figure that? Aren't you looking into this for Vera Shandy?"

R E S U R R E C T (twenty-five points)

"Honestly, I'm looking into it as much for myself as Vera. It's not like she hired me. She presented me with a mystery that she guessed, correctly, would interest me. If Eudora was involved, I'd kind of like to know."

"Sure about that?"

"Well...yes." Ellery had to ask. "Why? Do you think I'm going to find out Eudora was a murderess?"

He could hear the faint smile in Jack's, "I knew your aunt. Not well, but well enough to say I don't think you have anything to worry about there."

"It's pretty hard to believe, but maybe that's what everyone says when someone they know commits murder." Although maybe not members of the Shandy family?

"Pretty much," Jack agreed.

DOUBLEBLIND (nada points—how could that be?!).

Ellery closed the phone app.

"At least this time there's nothing riding on the outcome. No one is sitting in jail or even suffering through being suspected of committing murder. No one is being stalked or receiving death threats. There's no danger to anybody because it all went down over half a century ago. All the players are either deceased or pretty old. Even the remaining potential witnesses are elderly."

Jack's silence sounded unconvinced.

Ellery said coaxingly, "It's just a historical puzzle that would be interesting to solve, not least because it might lead to figuring out where those doubloons came from."

"And that's where the potential danger comes in," Jack said crisply. "If your calculations last night were even in the ballpark, that's a lot of motive. That's a million motives."

"What did the people from RIMAP say?"

"Too early to know for sure, but..."

"But?"

Jack said, "I spoke to RIMAP's head, Dr. Judith Shelton, and she said—off the record—the coins *appear* to be genuine."

"Wow."

"Yes."

Ellery absorbed that news for a moment, then returned to arguing his point. "That's amazing. *But* the treasure aspect is secondary."

"Maybe for you. Don't discount the lure of pirate's treasure for someone like Tackle Shandy."

"Sure, but it's not like I'm in possession of the coins. I have no clue where they came from, which I'm sure most people know."

"I get worried when you start making assumptions about what other people know or don't know. Or trust that because *you* would never do something, no one would."

Ellery said patiently, "I know that, Jack. I really do."

"Just remember, you're the one who suggested Vernon Shandy was murdered."

"Are you saying you *don't* think Vernon was murdered?"

Jack said somberly, "It's probable he was murdered, yes. But there's no evidence of that." He added, "Yet."

Ellery couldn't help smiling. "Is that a compliment?"

"A compliment is when I tell you what a great smile you have or how much I like hearing you sing in shower. I'm confident you'll come up with a plausible explanation for what happened back in '63. More than that, who knows." Jack's tone was hard to read. He did not sound overjoyed, that was for sure. But he wasn't trying to discourage Ellery from investigating, i.e., *poking his nose into other people's business.*

While Ellery was thinking that over, Jack changed the subject. "Are you staying in town tonight?"

Ellery said regretfully, "No. I'm waiting for the rain to ease up before I drive out to Captain's Seat. I need to check on the renovations, do some laundry, make sure my key still works." They usually spent Friday nights together. In fact, lately, they spent most nights together.

"Okay." Jack sounded a little disappointed, but he didn't offer to drive out to Captain's Seat, so maybe he needed a night to himself. Fair enough.

"With the library being painted, this is a great time to go through all those boxes of Eudora's books and maps."

"True."

"Speaking of which, I guess this explains why she had so many books on treasure hunting and pirate history. I just assumed she'd inherited those books the same way I did. It never occurred to me *she* was the treasure hunter."

Jack's laugh always made Ellery's heart lighten. "It makes sense, though, if you'd known her."

"I'm starting to regret never having the chance."

"You'd have liked her. She was one of a kind." Jack's tone changed, grew brisk, which Ellery knew meant someone had walked into his office. "Right. I'll talk to you later."

"Later."

Reluctantly, Ellery clicked off.

The drive from Pirate's Cove was a pretty and scenic thirty minutes, give or take, depending on road conditions. In the summer, those road conditions included idiots in golf carts and on mopeds and bicycles, who seemed to think the rules of the road didn't apply when you were on vacation. In the winter, the road conditions could be anything from a stray cow to a falling tree. Rain and sleet and snow were considerations, as was flooding.

But in autumn? The shadbush leaves turned golden and the winterberry shrubs lost their leaves, revealing tiny scarlet berries. The stone walls gleamed silver, and the wet fields, turned dark with rain, were dotted with wild mushrooms and white, blue, and purple asters. The wind-twisted trees tossed their gold and yellow leaves into the wind like joyful children throwing up their arms at the approaching holidays.

Last Christmas, Ellery's entire world had seemed to be crashing down around his ears. This Christmas, he would be meeting Jack's family.

Time and tide.

The rain had completely stopped by the time Ellery pulled into the small "courtyard" that served as the parking area in front of Captain's Seat. He parked and went around to open the door for Watson, who immediately took off for the back of the house, where he knew a family of squatter squirrels were hiding out. His shrill bark echoed off the slate-colored granite exterior and conical twin towers.

Arf! Arf! Arf!

The first time Ellery had seen Captain's Seat had been in a photo sent to him by Mr. Landry, Aunt Eudora's lawyer, and he'd laughed out loud. He'd thought for a second or two that Mr. Landry must be pulling his leg, although nothing about Mr. Landry up to that point (or afterward) indicated he was prone to jocularity.

But...*seriously?*

The place had looked like the mansion on the cover of a gothic suspense novel. Not that, at the time, Ellery had any idea what a gothic suspense novel was.

And when he'd finally seen the old mansion live and in technicolor? He'd felt a little light-headed. For one thing, it was so far from...anywhere. For another, it was obviously in terrible repair (and he didn't even know the half of it). And, last but not least, it was so big. What the heck was he supposed to do with a house the size of a small tenement?

His first instinct had been to sell. Take the money and run straight back to civilization.

But, for laughs, he'd decided to spend a night or two in ye olde baronial mansion, as it were, and, well, somehow the crazy white elephant of a house had grown on him.

Maybe it was the nuttiness of the galleon-themed interior architecture. Maybe it was the realization that Captain Horatio Page, the intimidating figure in the life-sized portrait hanging in the master bedroom, was actually *related* to him.

Maybe it was simply his desperation to escape the wreckage of his old life and start something, *anything*, new.

Anyway, he had stayed.

And now... The roses in the front garden—newly planted by himself and Jack—were in tentative bloom. The broken windows had all been replaced. A fresh new bed of glittering white gravel had been spread across the front drive. It wasn't going to make the front cover of *Home and Garden* anytime soon, but it had a certain world-weary elegance.

He whistled to Watson, who probably couldn't hear him over his barking, and went up the sparkling (that had been Jack wielding a pressure washer hose) steps to the front door.

He unlocked the door and stepped inside, making his way around drop cloths, saw horses, ladders, paint cans, and scattered tools.

"Hello? Anyone here?"

The workmen's vehicles were gone, so he would have been startled if anyone had answered.

The smell of paint and glue and saw dust and formaldehyde permeated the air as he wandered from room to room, checking out the progress.

As thrilled as he'd been by all that he and Jack had accomplished in the entry hall and kitchen, it was kind of awe-inspiring to see what an actual team of pros could do working for days on end.

One of the very coolest things that had happened so far was when the workmen had gone down to the cellar and discovered never used rolls of vintage wallpaper from the 1930s. The blue and silver paper featured delicate drawings of pairs of herons framed by acanthus and oak leaves in front of a mansion that looked remarkably like Captain's Seat.

The wallpaper was going onto the walls of Ellery's bedroom, although his room had not originally been included in the plans for renovation.

It was disconcerting how quickly you could burn through money when it came to things like tile and textiles.

But since the renovation was moving much more quickly now, Ellery had decided to hold a small house-warming party in November and invite some of his old friends.

A regular weekend house party.

Like in those Golden Age mysteries Nora was so fond of. Only minus the mystery. And *definitely* minus the murders.

With the exception of his parents (and Brandon), Ellery hadn't seen anyone from his old life since he'd left New York in February. He was looking forward to catching up with his old crew, hearing all the news, hearing all the gossip.

They would all continue to believe he'd had some kind of breakdown, but whatever.

Arf! Arf! Arf!

He glanced out the window. Daylight was fading rapidly into twilight, but there was still enough time for a quick walk down to the beach. It was tough on such an energetic young dog being cooped up in a bookshop all day. They could both use the exercise.

He went back outside, whistled to Watson who, this time, came galloping from behind the house as though it had never crossed his mind to start digging holes in that freshly planted bed of hydrangeas.

"Wanna go for a walk?" Ellery asked.

Watson considered that the best news he'd had all day. He jumped up and down and then took off like a shot across the drive and vanished into the field of tall grass and goldenrod. Ellery could hear him barking joyously into an ever-growing distance, but it was all right. There was no one to disturb. No humans, anyway. Even in the spring and summer, their nearest neighbors were out of sight and usually out of mind. And this time of year? There was literally no one in barking—or shouting—distance.

He waded through the wet field, drawing deep lungfuls of rain-sweet air. The tensions of the day—not that there were so many tensions these days—faded. Overhead, enormous, billowy, indigo-edged clouds shapeshifted into castles and galleons and formless, but mostly playful, monsters.

As he started down the steep hillside trail to the beach, he was conscious for the first time that Eudora—in fact, generations of Pages—must have taken these same paths many times, that he was literally following in the footsteps of his family, heck, his ancestors.

For the first time, he recognized what an amazing gift he had been given.

When he'd first arrived in Pirate's Cove, he'd been too busy trying to save the bookshop and the old house to focus on anything but what needed to be fixed, altered, updated. But now that things were starting to come together, he could appreciate not just what he had, but the possibilities for what could be.

He reached the sandy bottom of the hillside and walked along the water's edge, smiling as he watched Watson chasing away the waves, only to retreat, barking hysterically, when the tide came rushing back in noisy, foaming onslaught.

After locating a suitable piece of driftwood, Ellery played fetch with Watson for about ten minutes, and then, with the darkness closing in, they hiked back up the hillside, crossed the field, and walked up the drive to the house.

Ellery stopped in his tracks.

A light gleamed from one of the upstairs windows.

Okay. No big deal. One of the workmen must have left it on earlier in the day. Although, as far as Ellery could remember, that small room on the second floor was not included in the renovations.

Something about that single bright window made his scalp prickle.

What was that room anyway? A sitting room? Sewing room? Fainting room?

But seriously, what was the problem? He could have left the light on himself.

Except he never went in that chilly little room. It was kind of a depressing space, to be honest. He'd been considering knocking out the walls and adding onto one of the other bedrooms or turning it into another bathroom or something once he had a little extra cash in the bank.

A burglar would not turn the lights on. Someone lying in wait for him would not leave the lights on. Obviously one of the workmen had wandered up there for whatever reason and left a lamp on.

Which, truthfully, he wasn't crazy about the idea of workmen snooping through parts of the house they weren't supposed to be in, but that was still better than...

What?

Ghosts?

He laughed at himself and followed Watson up the steps, where he was waiting, tail wagging, for the next great thing to happen.

CHAPTER SEVEN

He was waist-high in dusty stacks of books when he remembered that Eudora had kept a diary.

Actually, it had been more combination daily record/appointment calendar/accounts ledger than what he thought of as a diary. Eudora had faithfully noted the weather conditions along with her blood pressure (which, given her age, had been excellent). She'd also used the book to file coupons, newspaper clippings that had no relevance to anything as far as Ellery could tell, and the occasional cartoon or poem. Once in a very great while she actually jotted down her thoughts or feelings, but mostly it was just a record of her, frankly, not very eventful life.

But, if Eudora had kept a regular diary as an old lady, wasn't it possible she'd started journaling as a young lady?

It was more than possible. It was highly probable.

What had he done with that old journal of hers?

He'd been cleaning out the master suite—not the most pleasant of tasks, if he was honest—when he'd come across it. He'd quickly flipped through the pages, feeling a little sad at how lonely Eudora's life looked from the outside (and even sadder when he reflected that he too was probably destined for a life of clipping out-of-date coupons and funny cat cartoons), and he'd put it aside…somewhere.

Where?

He wouldn't have tossed it. Even back then, when he'd felt no particular connection to the house or the people who'd once lived there, he wouldn't have discarded something like that.

So what would he have done with it?

It had to be here, somewhere in these piles of books and boxes. That would have been his thinking: it's book-shaped, put it with the other books.

He'd likely not find it until he'd finished sorting through all these books and maps and charts and ledgers.

In any case, that journal, the journal of Eudora's final year, wasn't going to be useful. She'd started the journal in January and she'd died in February.

Actually, none of those later journals—assuming they still existed—were going to be helpful.

What he needed was any kind of diary or calendar or notebook detailing Eudora's activities during the 1960s. Before or after 1963 would be useful, but if she'd actually kept a diary during the pivotal year of 1963, *that* could be a game changer. Not that he was expecting to discover something like *Pushed that bounder Vernon off Pequot Bluffs today.* For one thing, people didn't say *bounder* in 1963. If they ever really said it at all.

One thing about Eudora, she might have been an eccentric, but she was a meticulous record-keeping eccentric. She was also opinionated. If that journal existed, there was a high probability it was going to contain information pertinent to this case.

He hadn't come across Eudora's journal from the year before her death, so either she threw out the old journals when she started the new ones—and, given the fact that she didn't seem to throw *anything* out ever, that seemed unlikely—or she had stored her old journals somewhere.

The attic? The basement?

He'd never done more than glance inside the attic—that had been overwhelming enough—but the basement was crowded with trunks and boxes and crates and old furniture and creepy mirrors and cobwebbed portraits of alarming people who looked like they needed vitamin B shots STAT. The basement was probably the place to start his hunt.

He glanced out the window at the starry night sky. What time was it now? Eight? Nine? Watson snoozed peacefully atop an unopened box of books. Ellery checked his watch. *Ten?*

Yeah, no. Tomorrow would be soon enough for that adventure. If anyone knew better than to go down to the basement, it was the guy who'd barely survived eighteen visits to basements in the six *Happy Halloween! You're Dead* films.

Which reminded him. He hadn't told Jack about the unexpected opportunity (Was it an opportunity? He couldn't quite decide) to take part in the *Happy Halloween* reboot.

But then, he wasn't sure he wanted to bring it up to Jack until he had worked out how *he* felt about it.

For one thing, who would take care of Watson while he was gone?

"Hey, buddy," he said softly. "It's bedtime."

Watson opened one eye, gave one of those all-engulfing Muppet yawns, and nearly fell off the box.

Ellery chuckled, scooped him up, but Watson suddenly came to full attention, wriggling furiously until Ellery put him down. The pup raced out of the room, tags jingling, and Ellery raised his head, listening.

He also recognized the rumble of that particular engine, the crunch of gravel beneath those particular tires, that particular police radio cutting off mid-crackle.

He sprinted to the front door, though hopefully with more dignity than Watson, who was scratching to be let out.

When he opened the door, Watson flew down the steps and charged Jack, who was making his way across the moonlight walk. The rain-washed night air was sparkling clear and sharply cold. The smell of damp earth and wet leaves mingled with the faraway tang of the sea.

Ellery followed, watching Jack field Watson's leap into his arms.

Jack grunted. "He's getting too big for this. It's like catching a cannon ball."

"Believe me, it's worse if you miss." He reached Jack, who exchanged an armful of Watson for an armful of Ellery. "Hello, you." He kissed Ellery.

"Hiya. I didn't think you were coming."

Jack kissed him again, lightly. "I wasn't sure I could get away."

"Underpromise, overdeliver. That's you."

"I try."

Ellery stopped walking, staring upward. Jack, his arm around Ellery's shoulders, stopped too. "What's up?"

"That light's on again."

They stared silently up at the shining window on the second floor.

"What room is that?"

"I'm not sure. It's like a little reading room or sitting room. There must be a short in that lamp."

"Unplug it. The last thing you need is another fire."

"That's for sure." His flash of unease forgotten, Ellery led the way into the house. "Are you hungry? Can I fix you something to eat?"

"I grabbed a club sandwich for dinner. I wouldn't mind a beer."

"I can make that happen."

They went inside, Ellery got Jack a Grey Sail IPA, and gave him a quick tour of the renovations thus far. Jack approved the newly discovered vintage wallpaper, admired the new chandelier light fixture in the dining room, and seemed genuinely awestruck by the work done refinishing and varnishing the steps, stair rails, and banisters built to look like the row of cannons on the broadside of a warship.

"I kind of like the look of the windows without drapes," Ellery was saying as they started up to the second floor. "I like the light through those tall, narrow windows. I even like the moonlight."

"This far from the village there shouldn't be a problem with Peeping Toms."

Ellery did a doubletake. "Does the village have a problem with Peeping Toms?"

"Occasionally. Over the years," Jack replied. "What will you do with the mermaid?"

The mermaid was a nine-foot-long scratched and peeling ship's figurehead that had previously hung over the runway-length dining table.

"Move her to the library where there's less chance she'll be taking out half my friends in one blow."

They reached the small room on the second floor. The door was open, and the room was dark.

"That lamp's got a short for sure," Ellery remarked, finding his way across the room. He found the little table with the glass lamp, knelt, and unplugged the cord from the wall socket.

"This room is *really* cold," Jack said from right over-head, and Ellery jumped. Jack made a sound of amusement. "You're jumpy tonight."

Ellery chuckled, but his heart was jerking around in his chest. Silly though it was, something about this room made him uneasy. Even Jack's featureless silhouette standing over him made him nervous.

He rose, moving back toward the doorway and the lighted hall, where Watson waited for them. "Do you smell roses?"

Jack sniffed a couple of times. "No. I smell carpet, sawn wood, and adhesive."

Ellery sniffed too and admitted, "I don't smell it now. I must be imagining things."

Jack patted his back.

Jack had a second beer, and they were on the sofa in front of the cozy fire in the wide room that had once been the front parlor, when Ellery offered Jack the printout of his list of suspects.

Jack raised his eyebrows, set his beer glass on the floor next to the sleeping furball that was Watson, and took the printout.

He read, "Joey (Josephine) Franklin. No idea who that is. Ditto Douglas Franklin. Rocky Shandy..." He gave a short laugh. "Okay. Maybe. If Rocky did it, he probably doesn't remember."

"Great. Do you think he could have been capable of murder?"

"I think Tackle is a chip off the old block, if that tells you anything."

It told him Rocky had been a thug, a bully, and not overly concerned with breaking the law. It might or might not indicate a capacity for murderous violence.

"Was Rocky ever in prison?"

"Prison? No. He spent some time in jail, but that was mostly petty stuff. Largely related to caught being a dumbass while drinking."

"Was he another treasure hunter?"

"The entire family are treasure hunters in one form or another." Jack's tone was sardonic.

"Well, they're descended from wreckers, so maybe it's in their genes."

"Maybe. But I wouldn't advise anyone trying to use that in their legal defense."

Jack returned his attention to the list. "Barry Shandy was way before my time. I think he was one of the brothers who earned a Navy Cross in World War II."

"War heroes?"

"Yep. Tony Bernard…never heard of him." He continued to read and then glanced at Ellery. "Eudora Page is still on the list? You seriously consider your aunt a suspect?"

The logs in the fireplace gave a hissing sound. The fire popped, showering glowing sparks, which swirled in the draft before vanishing up the chimney. Watson hastily transferred from the floor to the sofa next to Ellery, from where he warily watched the fireplace.

"Vera seriously considers her a suspect, so in the interest of fairness, I guess I have to at least consider the possibility."

Jack studied Ellery. "And what if you find out Eudora was guilty?"

"I'm not going to be happy, I can tell you that. But I think Vera deserves to know the truth. And I think Eudora deserves to have her name cleared."

"I agree. I'm glad you see it that way." Jack's mouth curved in a faint smile. "I already told you what I think."

Ellery admitted, "Maybe that's why I'm not afraid to investigate her."

Jack grinned, tightened the arm around Ellery's shoulders, drawing him closer. He kissed him, and Ellery settled his head on Jack's shoulder. Watson settled his head on Ellery's thigh.

"So what did you think of Vera?" Jack asked.

"Not what I expected."

"Don't underestimate her."

"No. I won't."

"Vera's sole allegiance is to her family."

"I believe it. She's on my list. Well, the list I keep in my head."

Jack gave a quiet laugh. "You must show me that filing system sometime."

"You don't think Vera could commit murder?"

"She's capable, you're right about that. Cool-headed, nerves of steel, a fast thinker. But she's also smart and practical. I think Vera would also find a smarter, safer way to deal with an enemy. Also, like I said, family is always first with Vera. It would take a lot for Vera to kill one of her own."

"A fortune in pirate's gold?"

"More than that, I think."

Ellery tended to think Jack was right.

For a few minutes neither spoke, the only sounds the fire's song, the wind whispering outside, and the squeaks and creaks of a very old house settling down to sleep.

"Any word from Dylan?" Jack asked quietly.

Ellery shook his head. Dylan Carter was perhaps his closest friend in Pirate's Cove. He owned the Toy Chest, the charming little toy and games store right next to the Crow's Nest, and he ran the local amateur theater guild known as the Scallywags.

"The break will do him good."

Ellery nodded again but said nothing. After the events of the previous month, his loyalties were a little divided. He understood and sympathized wholeheartedly with Dylan's feelings. But he also understood Jack's point of view. Either way, he missed Dylan, and he missed the Monday Night Scrabblers.

"Then no Monday game night?" Jack questioned.

"No." Ellery gave him a sideways look. "The Silver Sleuths are holding an emergency meeting. All hands on deck."

Jack closed his eyes as if in great pain, and Ellery snickered.

"Don't worry. I'll keep a close eye on them."

Jack shook his head. "The touching innocence of you imagining you have *any* control over those maniacs."

"You have to admit, they've been pretty helpful a few times."

"Oh no. No, I don't have to admit anything like that. Maybe, *maybe* they've somehow been helpful to you, but they've not been helpful to me."

Ellery grinned. "Have *I* been helpful to you?"

Jack turned his head to nuzzle Ellery. He said softly, "*You*, Mr. Page, are a whole different story."

CHAPTER EIGHT

"If I drop this, you'll be sleeping in a dog house from here on out," muttered the voice in his dreams.

Ellery frowned, tried to weave that dialogue into the pleasant scenario that had been developing a moment or two before, but the alarming *rattle* of crockery, *clink* of silverware, and *creak* of straining wood dissipated the last delightful wisps.

His nose twitched, his eyelids fluttered, his lips parted, and a warm mouth gently, sweetly pressed his own once, twice—only to be rudely shoved aside by a long, whiskery snout panting sweet nothings into his face before covering him in eager licks.

He started to laugh—which was a tactical error.

"*Hey*, no...*ewww*...stop..."

"Watson!" Jack airlifted the offender. "For God's sake."

Ellery sat up only to be knocked back into the pillows as Watson eluded his would-be captor and pounced, delighted and desperate. Ellery laughed. "Okay, okay. Good morning to you too."

He grinned up at Jack. "And good morning to you."

"Not the way I planned this." Jack, hands on hips, studied the picture of Watson lying atop Ellery.

Now that Kingston was running Saturday Storytime, Ellery was able to go into work a bit later, giving him and

Jack a few precious extra hours together on Saturday mornings.

"Don't give up so easily. Tell me what you planned." Ellery sat up, dislodging Watson, and caught sight of the large breakfast tray sitting on the bureau between the windows. His eyes widened.

"Yikes. You made breakfast." The *yikes* was because Jack was really not a very good cook. In fact, he was kind of terrible. It was pretty much the only thing he was not good at, but when it came to being bad, he was really good. Anyway, it was a lovely, thoughtful gesture. Ellery beamed.

"I figured it was my turn to make *you* breakfast." Jack retrieved the heavy tray and lowered it carefully to the bed, while Ellery stacked the pillows behind him.

"This looks fantastic." That blob of egg and...milky mustard?...did truly look like something not of this world. "W-what is it?"

"Eggs Benedict."

"*Is* it? Gosh. To what do I owe this honor?"

Jack shrugged, looking uncharacteristically self-conscious, so he must have tried very hard to get it right. He'd gone all out too, dragging out the good china, the fragile stuff from the 1920s with the bluebirds and apple blossoms pattern. He'd chopped up a lot of random fruit and sprinkled it with sugar—so much sugar—and those little charred twigs had probably once been bacon.

Jack sat on the side of bed, facing Ellery. His expression was earnest and sort of uncertain.

"Aren't you having any of this?" Ellery asked.

"No. It's all for you."

"At least have a piece of bacon."

Jack took the blackened strip but then just held it between his fingers—not seeming to notice when Watson ever so delicately took it from him.

"Hey." Ellery scowled at Watson. Watson looked appropriately chastened for about two seconds and then gazed hopefully at Jack.

Jack drew in a sharp breath as though waking from a trance. "It's funny because we really haven't known each other that long—"

"Eight months." Ellery considered that. "Although, I'm not sure we can count before we were actually dating."

"I think we can. We were getting to know each other."

"I was getting to know that you really take parking citations and construction-code violations seriously," Ellery teased.

Jack sighed. Heavily. *"Anyway—"*

"Sorry. Anyway?"

"These last few months have—"

Jack's cell phone rang. Jack groaned and swore, which was really not at all like him. Jack was stamped from the *I could not love thee (Dear) so much, Lov'd I not Honour more* mold.

He threw Ellery a look of frustration and snatched his phone up. "Carson."

On the other end of the call, an animated mosquito began to explain the situation that required yanking Pirate's Cove chief of police out of bed at ten a.m. on a Saturday morning.

"At their age?" Jack protested.

Watson padded up to inspect the breakfast tray. Ellery pushed him back with a stern whisper. "You know better." He mouthed, *At least, wait until he's gone.*

Watson wagged his tail, offered his best puppy eyes.

Kind of disheartening to think his dog was a better actor than he was.

"Oh for—!" Jack clipped out, "On my way," and clicked off. He gazed at Ellery with resignation. "Domestic disturbance."

"*Argh*," Ellery said. Or similar sounds of despair and disappointment. "And the *chief of police* has to settle it?"

"They're asking for me."

"Who is?"

Jack hesitated, admitted, "The Crawfords."

"The—" Ellery broke off, staring. "Bess and Abel Crawford? They're like a hundred years old!"

"He is. She's one hundred and two."

"And they still haven't figured out how to get along?"

"I don't know what to tell you." Jack made a face. "Except I'm sorry. I was looking forward to having the morning together."

Ellery let out a long, measured breath. He had known going into this relationship that there were challenges dating a cop. He was determined to always be supportive and patient. Besides, he expected Jack to be understanding about his little amateur sleuthing hobby. The least he could do was be understanding about Jack's actual job.

"That's okay. There'll be other mornings." He winked. "And nights."

To his surprise, Jack groaned again.

Ellery laughed. "I'm starting to think you need a vacation."

"I need a…" Jack swallowed the rest of it.

"Back rub? Steak dinner? Stiff drink? Come back tonight, and I'll provide all three."

Jack shook his head, though he wasn't declining the invitation because he muttered, "I'm definitely coming back tonight."

Ellery reached for him. "Sounds good. Until then, how about a kiss goodbye?"

* * * * *

Nora and Kingston were hanging old-fashioned paper jack-o'-lantern garlands and bickering amiably when Ellery and Watson arrived at the Crow's Nest just before lunchtime.

"Those look great. Where'd you find them?"

"They were in the cellar," Nora informed him. "In the box you marked *Decorations*."

"Oh. Right." Those first few weeks of shoveling out the bookshop from years of Great-great-great-aunt Eudora's hoarding were a blur of dust, cobwebs, and disintegrating paperbacks. "Better late than never. How did Saturday Storytime go?"

"Very well," Nora said. "Kingston read *In a Dark, Dark Wood* by David A. Carter. In honor of Halloween."

"Good choice." Frankly, Ellery had never heard of three-quarters of the books Kingston chose for Saturday Storytime, but that was a title he could remember his mother reading to him when he'd been very young.

"The children loved it." Nora smiled at Kingston.

Kingston smiled at Nora.

"I'm going to check my email," Ellery said.

Arf, Watson concurred.

"Wait," Nora said. "Did Chief Carson tell you whether there's been any progress on the case?"

"What case?"

Nora was rarely confused, but she looked confused then. "You mean he's not opening a homicide investigation into Vernon Shandy's death?"

"Nora, there's no proof that Vernon's even dead. *We* think he's dead. His family thinks he's dead. But Jack would need more than that to open an investigation. For one thing, the family hasn't asked him to. The Navy doesn't think he's dead. Their official view is he deserted."

"But what about the pirate doubloons?"

"We know how the doubloons got in my office. We know how they got onto the *Roussillon*. Vera claimed the collection bag and doubloons belonged to Vernon, but she didn't admit knowledge of how that collection bag and diving suit wound up in the Historical Society's warehouse."

"It's inferred, dearie."

"Implied," Kingston murmured.

"Well, yes, but also inferred. By us. Which was Vera's expectation."

"Ah. Of course."

"*Anyway,*" Ellery broke in, "the point of *our* investigation is to put together enough evidence to convince Jack to open a real investigation."

Nora frowned. "I do feel our investigations have held *some* validity, some merit in their own right."

"Yes, of course. I think we've been helpful, which is why Jack—"

"I think we've been *more* than helpful! I think without us—er, you—"

"I don't mind sharing the blame."

"Many of these cases would have gone unsolved."

"I wouldn't go that far."

Nora said stubbornly, "I would. And further."

Ellery glanced at Kingston, who had diplomatically removed himself from the fray. He was positioning a papier-mâché black cat in a party hat on the sales desk.

Ellery sighed. "Okay, well, hopefully we'll be helpful and more this time too. Now, I'm just going to go—"

"Sue Lewis phoned," Nora called after him.

Ellery turned warily. "Why?"

"She wants to know if you'd be willing to be interviewed regarding your discovery of the gold doubloons."

"No. Way."

Nora said patiently, "It's a good story. Sue's not wrong for wanting to pursue it. That's her job, after all."

"No way," Ellery repeated. "I know exactly how it would go. No matter what I said, I'd come out of that interview looking like *I'd* killed Vernon Shandy for the treasure. It won't matter that I wasn't born yet. She'll think that looks *more* suspicious."

Kingston tried to cover his laugh with a cough.

Nora said, "Don't you think that after everything that's happened, that perhaps you and Sue could put the past behind you?"

"Sure," Ellery said. "I'm happy to put the past behind me. But that doesn't mean I have to give her interviews. I don't trust her."

Nora did not go so far as to tsk-tsk, but she clearly disapproved of Ellery's attitude. Well, that was fine for Nora. She hadn't been the target of one of Sue's smear campaigns.

Ellery continued into his office, settled behind his desk, turned on the desktop to check his email, quickly scrolling through the usual pleas for money and promises of male enhancement and mystery inheritances—been there, done that, thankyouverymuch—in search of the occasional query from a genuine customer looking for a genuine book.

No one seemed to be in need of a book hunter, however. Or even a bookseller.

Which was why he worried about how the Crow's Nest would fare during those long off-season months. Which was one reason why he was still considering Ronny's proposal.

His cell phone rang.

It took him a moment to recognize Felix's cell phone number.

"Hey! How's it going? How are things at Brown?" Felix had started college in Providence the previous month.

"It's great," Felix said, and he sounded genuinely happy and more relaxed than he had in a long time. "It's nice starting fresh where no one knows anything about you."

No one but Libby, presumably, but Ellery didn't ask. Libby and Felix's relationship was none of his business.

"I feel you," he said, and Felix chuckled, although the traumatic events he wanted to put behind him were very different from Ellery's.

Ellery listened for a couple of minutes to Felix rattle on about his courses and his professors—he was majoring in Theater Arts and Performance Studies—and about how much he loved Providence. It sounded like everything was going very well, so that was good news.

He put in the occasional *That's great!* when required, and eventually he managed to break in. "Hey, so do you remember when I asked you about Cap Murphy giving you a diving bag he thought I'd left on the *Fishful Thinking*?"

"Uh, yeah. Sure." Felix sounded cautious.

"I found the bag in the back of the storage cabinet."

"Oh. Okay. So that's good, right?"

"Yes. It's just you thought you'd left the bag out on the shelves."

There was silence on the other end of the line, and then Felix said doubtfully, "Is something missing from the bag?"

"No. Well, I have no idea, really. I just…" Ellery began to feel foolish, but it was about establishing provenance, right? "Do you think you could have put it in the cupboard instead of leaving it out?"

"I must have. I don't remember doing anything with it, to be honest. I was crazy-busy and trying to get out of there to meet Libby. I probably had second thoughts about leaving the bag where anyone could find it."

That made sense. Ellery remembered being twenty.

"Did anything happen to make you uneasy that evening? Was anyone hanging around?"

Felix's tone brightened. "You know what? Yeah. Ned Shandy's uncle was circling the place like a vulture."

"Tackle? Is that who you mean?"

"Yeah. The one who did jail time for manslaughter. I thought he was there for me."

"For *you*?"

"Because Ned and I had that blow up over Libby." Felix gave a short laugh. "I thought Tackle was going to put his two cents in, but by the time I locked up, he was gone."

"I see," Ellery said thoughtfully. He was pretty sure he did.

Felix waited a moment or two before asking, "Was that it? Because I should get going. We've got our dress rehearsal for *The Birthday Party* this afternoon."

Ellery was unclear if Felix was referring to the play by Pinter or another social event. Anyway, he had what he needed. "Okay. Well, break a leg. Unless you're really going to a party, in which case, don't break any legs."

Felix chuckled, said, "Say hi to everybody," and hung up.

CHAPTER NINE

Let's start at the very beginning

A very good place to start

Somehow, he'd got that earworm from *The Sound of Music* coiled in his brain.

Not that it was bad advice. Actually, it was pretty good advice.

Ellery began his hunt for Josephine and Douglas Franklin with a search of Pirate Cove's online directory.

There was no listing for Josephine Franklin and no listing for Douglas Franklin. There *was* a listing for a James Franklin.

Not a lot of Franklins on Buck Island, so maybe James was a relative of Josephine and Douglas? Maybe not. Just in case he was, Ellery decided it would be wise to find out a bit more about the Franklins before he started asking awkward questions. Especially since at this stage he had no idea what to ask.

Hey, did you or anyone in your family kill Vernon Shandy back in 1963? was probably not going to get the best results.

Online directories were often incomplete, so maybe he could go old-school and look in the physical phone directory for Buck Island.

Ellery dug the phone directory out from beneath a stack of old *Alfred Hitchcock Mystery Magazines* and flipped to the *F*s.

Again, the only Franklin on Buck Island seemed to be James Franklin living on New Harbor Lane. Those homes were of relatively recent construction, so it was possible James was a newcomer to the island.

On impulse, he rose and went to the storage cupboard which, come to think of it, he'd never finished clearing out, and began digging around for an older version of the phone directory. He had a vague memory...

Ah. Yes. There it was. Actually, there were several, including 1985, 1986, 1990, and 2000.

Ellery dragged the directories out, dropped them on his desk with a *thump*, and began scanning listings under *F*.

In 2000, James had been living (still on his own, it seemed) in the house on New Harbor Lane. There was no record of any other Franklins on the island.

But in the 1990 directory... Bingo.

Back in the early nineties, Mrs. D. Franklin had been living on High Street. There was no listing at all for James Franklin. So, either James Franklin had not yet arrived on the island, or he had been living with his mom.

Was there another explanation? Ellery couldn't think of one off-hand.

Mrs. D. Franklin...

If the Franklins had divorced, surely the former missus would not still be listing herself as Mrs. D. Franklin? Besides, there ought to be a separate listing somewhere for Douglas. Unless he'd left the island?

He'd left the island all right. Ellery's guess was that by 1990, Josephine was a widow. A widow living with her son.

He turned to 1986. Same story. The widowed Mrs. Franklin was living with her son on High Street. Those houses on High Street were expensive, but back in the day, they'd been medium-priced homes well within the reach of a working-class family with an average income, let alone two incomes, assuming that Josephine continued to work through 1990. He was drawing a lot of conclusions based on a couple of lines in an out-of-date phone book.

Ellery moved on to the phone book for 1985.

Aha!

There was only one change, but it was significant: in 1985, Mr. *and* Mrs. D. Franklin had been living in the house on High Street. So Douglas had died either late 1985 or early 1986. Josephine had passed sometime in the 1990s.

Long after Vernon had mysteriously disappeared, the Franklins had continued to reside and work in Pirate's Cove, living perfectly ordinary-seeming lives.

Would they do that if they had any involvement in Vernon's disappearance?

Not that Ellery had any firsthand experience, but if it were him, he'd try to get as far away from the scene of the crime as he soon as he safely could.

He left his office and returned to the book floor. Kingston had not yet returned from lunch, but he found Nora muttering to herself in the Thriller section.

"Do you know anything about a James Franklin?"

Nora's reply, as she returned abandoned books to their rightful shelves, sounded absent. "The Penn State football coach?"

"No. At least, that seems doubtful. I can only find one listing for Franklin on the entire island, and that's James Franklin."

"It's not a common name on the island," Nora admitted. "Off the top of my head, I really can't recall knowing any Franklins."

"You said you thought Josephine might have been the waitress at the Deep Dive."

"She might have been. At fourteen, I wasn't a regular."

"You're not a regular now. Nor the Salty Dog either."

"I'm not much for spirits," Nora admitted.

Ellery teased, "For which I suspect we should all be grateful."

"My dear mother used to always say: 'In temperance there is ever cleanliness and elegance.'"

"Mine says: 'The problem with the world is that everyone is a few drinks behind.'"

Nora chuckled. "I believe your mother is cribbing from Humphrey Bogart."

"Mm-hm. My ma is the Humphrey Bogart of serious actresses."

Nora laughed again and put the final stray book on the final shelf.

The brass bell chimed, and sea air wafted down the aisles of books, so either they finally had customer or Kingston was back from lunch. Judging by the barometer of Watson's wagging tail, it was Kingston.

"Nora, how is it possible you don't know *anything* about these people?"

Nora said defensively, "After all, dearie, there are four thousand people on this island. I can't know *all* of them."

"I don't see why not," Ellery replied. "You've known everyone so far."

"Maybe they moved away from the island?" Kingston suggested, joining them.

"I'm pretty sure Douglas and Josephine have moved away from everything and everywhere. Permanently."

"*Oh.*" Nora and Kingston exchanged uneasy looks.

Nora said, "Of course, you could always check the morgue."

"The..." Ellery stared at her.

Kingston said kindly, "I believe Nora means the newspaper morgue."

"Don't be so sure," Ellery told him. "Anyway, when did Sue Lewis start publishing the *Scuttlebutt Weekly*? I thought the paper was only a few years old?"

"Before the *Scuttlebutt Weekly* there was the *Yardarm*," Nora informed him. When Sue started the *Scuttlebutt Weekly*, she acquired most of the *Yardarm*'s assets, including their morgue. She archives all the old bound volumes of newspapers with the *Scuttlebutt*'s. Which is very generous of her. In fact, she's said she ultimately intends to have both physical archives scanned and digitized."

"I never said she was all bad." Ellery contemplated this potentially valuable resource. The problem was, visiting that newspaper morgue was liable to mean running into Sue, something he'd prefer not to do. Call him chicken, but Ellery did not like confrontation, and he'd already had enough confrontations with Sue to last him a lifetime.

As though reading his thoughts, Kingston suggested, "The local library also has microfilm copies of the island's newspapers pre-2000. What if I tackle our list of suspects from that angle?"

"Excellent thought." Nora's gray eyes shone with approval and admiration.

"Agreed. Maybe there's a way we can get access to the Deep Dive's employment records?" Ellery was thinking aloud. "Vera should be able to get me access."

"Ah." Nora sounded regretful. "There might be a hitch. The original Deep Dive burned down in 1965."

"You mean the Deep Dive on Coral Avenue isn't the same Deep Dive where Josephine and Douglas worked?"

"They may very well have worked both locations. I'm sure most of the staff did."

"Most of the staff would be Shandy family members," Ellery pointed out.

"Yes. And I don't know that the change of location is relevant, except it might not be easy to access the old employment records if they were lost in the fire."

"Right." Ellery frowned. "Well, Vera made up the list of suspects, so she should be able to fill in some of the blanks for me."

"She didn't explain her reasoning behind listing each name?"

"Not really. She's been brooding over Vernon's disappearance for decades. I'm guessing she's been moving suspects on and off that list for years."

"That's probably true. In fact, it lends credence to this whittled-down list."

"Because she's had plenty of time to consider and reconsider all the players," Ellery concluded.

"Exactly. Vera's no fool. She might not have actual evidence, let alone proof, but if someone's on that list, they've landed there with good reason."

"Including Eudora?"

Nora's gaze veered from his and returned to the neatened bookshelf. "She knew you'd take the case once you saw Eudora's name. For all we know, she added Eudora's name simply to lure you in."

"You think she was lying about my aunt's friendship with Vernon?"

Nora looked thoughtful. She said slowly, "No. No, they were good friends. I do remember that. I don't think I fully understood the nature of their friendship back then."

"Maybe there was nothing to understand. Maybe they were just pals."

Nora considered, gave a slight shake of her head. "They were pals, yes. But I think they had to be more than pals." She glanced at him. "You could see it in the way they joked with each other. And in the way they argued. Really, you could see it in the very way they stood next to each other. As though they were touching even when they were feet apart."

"Hm." Ellery decided to let that go. Nora had doubtlessly been a little smarty-pants, but she'd still only been fourteen years old. Her lack of experience had to color her interpretations. Never mind the fact that after nearly sixty years, she was bound to have forgotten a few things. Heck, he forgot things from last week.

He asked instead, "Where was the original Deep Dive located?"

"On the other side of the harbor."

"But there's nothing over there."

"Not anymore, but at one time, nearly one third of the village was situated on the far side of Old Harbor." Nora glanced at Kingston, who nodded agreement.

"There used to be several shops and businesses all centered around the Royale," Kingston explained.

"What was the Royale?"

"A very grand hotel built in 1915. In its day it was quite the vacation destination. The Royale had its own private beach, a ballroom, and a first-class dining room that could seat twelve hundred people."

Nora nodded eagerly. "My parents used to go to dances there. And I remember as a little girl having lunch in that amazing dining room. There was nothing like it on the island, before or since."

Kingston said, "Granted, by 1965, the Royale had fallen into serious disrepair and was no longer much in use."

Nora said, "But the rest of the shops and businesses were still thriving."

"Yes."

"You're kidding," Ellery said, although it was obvious from their expressions they weren't.

Nora said, "No. The fire in 1965 was the greatest disaster to ever befall the island."

"How is it I've never heard anything about this fire until this past week?"

"Amazingly, no one was killed." Nora shrugged. "And what doesn't kill you, leaves others little to talk about."

CHAPTER TEN

"I found her!" Nora announced.

Ellery looked up from reading Tony Bernard's online obituary. Vernon's Navy diving buddy and best pal had been killed in a covert operation off Vietnam in 1967. Bernard had left behind two grieving parents and a fiancée: Miss Vera Shandy of Pirate's Cove, Buck Island, RI.

The information came courtesy of a distant niece of Tony's, who had posted her entire family history on a public website for the edification and entertainment of all. It was unsettling what the love for genealogy could do to a person.

Ellery had been frowning over why Vera would have named her former fiancé as a possible suspect in her brother's disappearance when Nora popped her head in the doorway.

"Who?" Ellery asked blankly.

"Josephine Franklin."

"Isn't she—" Ellery was going to say *dead*—he had already concluded Josephine had moved on to that island in the sky—but Nora said, "She's still living in Pirate's Cove."

"She *is*?"

"She's at Sunset Shores."

"What the heck is Sunset Shores?"

"A residential facility for elders. Actually, it's the island's only residential facility for elders."

Ellery said, "Every day I learn something new."

"It's fairly small and relatively expensive. Most families here keep their senior loved ones at home. But it's not always possible. And it's not always preferable. Not everyone wants to room with their children and grandchildren."

"True. I guess."

"Anyway, she was thrilled. She can see you this afternoon."

"*What?* When?" Ellery rose, dislodging Watson, who was sleeping beneath the desk, with his head on Ellery's foot. "It's already the afternoon!"

"Three o'clock. That leaves you plenty of time to get there. Also, she said to bring her a carton of cigarettes."

"She— To a nursing home?"

"Assisted living, dearie. They're not exactly the same thing. But yes, you're quite right. It's a no-smoking facility."

"Then why—what did you tell her?"

Nora's smile was composed. "That you wouldn't be late for your appointment. She doesn't have all the time in the world, you know."

Ellery, halfway out the door, threw her an uneasy look. "Yikes. A little cold, Nora."

"People my age are realists. Now remember, your name is Elliot Parker."

Ellery halted mid-step and turned to face her. "CUT. You gave her my stage name? Why?"

Nora looked at him as though he were the ninny Vera had claimed. "Because we don't want to give your real name."

"But I always give my real name. Why the subterfuge?"

"If Eudora Page really was Josephine's romantic rival, she might not wish to reveal her darkest secrets to Eudora's nephew."

Not a bad point. Still Ellery felt obliged to say, "She's not going to reveal her darkest secrets to a complete stranger either."

"You've never been to one of those places, have you, dearie? I assure you, Josephine will be *delighted* to spill the tea to a handsome, personable young man. *Especially* a handsome, personable young man working on a book about the island's unsolved mysteries."

Ellery said slowly, "I'd be lying if I pretended it doesn't concern me how easily you come up with these fabrications."

"Nonsense." Nora made shooing motions. "Hurry up! Don't be late. And *be charming.*"

Unlike most of Buck Island's forthright and hardworking New England architecture, Sunset Shores seemed to have been modeled on a villa vacationing in the south of France.

Surrounded by needle palm trees and surprisingly lush tropical gardens, the creamy-colored stucco single-story building featured an angled tile roof and an interplay of solid walls and colonnades opening into large spaces with enormous windows and sliding doors to create the illusion of living within the garden.

Which, frankly, was something Ellery had never longed to do, though he could see how residents of an assisted living facility might have different view. Literally.

In his opinion, Sunset Shores was about as unhomey as a place could be, and clean to the point of sterility. The air in the reception lobby was scented with a peculiar blend of bleach, disinfectant, and tropical air freshener. That said, they were expecting him at the front desk, and he was greeted pleasantly and whisked straight to Mrs. Franklin's room without delay.

His escort, a young woman in pink scrubs, tapped discreetly on the half-open door and called, "Joey, Mr. Parker is here."

"Send him in!" ordered a raspy, sexless voice.

The young woman pushed the door wide, nodded to Ellery in what was clearly *good luck, bucko!* and departed hastily on soundless, rubber-soled feet.

Ellery entered the room, which turned out to be an unexpectedly light and airy suite. It took him a second or two to pick out Josephine from the piles of throw pillows on the sofa and chairs. A tiny, gaunt woman seated in the corner of the sofa, leaned slightly forward, braced on her cane, watching him with bright black button eyes. She was as wrinkled as a mummy, but her talon-length nails were freshly manicured in aqua blue. She wore scarlet lipstick, false eyelashes, and an obvious wig in an expensive shade of ash blonde.

All of which sounded pretty ghastly, but in fact, the general effect was just sort of…whimsical.

"Where the hell are my cigarettes?" Joey greeted him.

"Sorry. They frisked me on the way in," Ellery lied. He held up a bouquet of yellow roses. "I managed to get these through, though."

Josephine threw her head back and cackled. "I believe it! I believe it! Those damn spoilsports!"

(She didn't say *spoilsports*, by the way, but you already knew that.)

"Thank you so much for agreeing to see me, Mrs. Franklin."

She waved that off. "Call me Joey, everyone does. You can use the flower vase in the cabinet beneath the wet bar."

Ellery threw her a quick look, and she cackled again. "Well, *I* call it a wet bar."

Ellery found the flower vase, filled it with water, and added the flowers.

"You can put them here on the table beside me. I love roses. My son James always brings houseplants. Like I want to be bothered taking care of a moth orchid." She winked, cocked her head, inspecting Ellery. "My, my, *my*. How tall are you?"

"Six feet."

"You're a nice-looking young feller."

"You're very kind."

Josephine snorted. "There's a first for everything. You can sit right there. So, your assistant said you're writing a book. You don't look much like an author."

Ellery seated himself on a chair so low to the ground, it felt like he was squatting. "It's my first book. I probably won't start looking like an author until my third or fourth."

She laughed, but it was automatic, as though her mind were on something else. "What made you choose Buck Island of all places?"

"Uh...distant family connections. My dad used to spend summers here when he was a kid. And, you know, pirates."

"Pirates!" Her expression was sardonic. "One of our natural resources. Boys love pirates, that's the truth. So what unsolved mystery do you think I can help you with?"

Perhaps Nora was wearing off on him because Ellery said glibly, "I thought I'd end the book with a story from the 1960s. The world was changing, the island was changing, and this particular unsolved mystery straddles both the old world and the new."

"Vernon's treasure," she said with sudden weariness.

"Right. Exactly."

"Who told you about me and Vernon?" Joey's black pebble gaze never wavered from his face.

In this case, honesty seemed like the best policy. "His sister Vera."

Joey scowled. "I hope you're not relying on the word of that b-i-t-c-h."

(Puzzlingly, she did indeed spell out the word.)

"Rely? No. But Vera does have an interesting story to tell."

"I don't doubt that! She always had interesting stories to tell. They're called lies. She *never* liked me. Always found fault with my work. And that was before Vern and I got involved. The nerve of *that* woman looking down on *me*."

"It seems like people either love her or hate her."

"Mostly they hate her," Joey said. "Speaking on behalf of everyone who worked for her, past, present, and future. I can't believe the b-i-t-c-h is still alive and kicking."

(What was the deal with the spelling? Did she think there was someone listening in who lacked a sixth-grade reading vocabulary?)

Ellery tried to gently steer her away from past grievances. "I guess you must have met Vernon when you were working at the Deep Dive?"

"That's right. The first time I ever saw him, he was home on leave. He walked into the pub, looking like a million bucks in that uniform. Well, you must've seen the photos of him. He was so handsome."

"I actually haven't seen any photos of him yet."

Joey looked surprised. "You haven't? Vera must have drawers full of them. She carried that little Brownie camera around all the time she wasn't working, which was *all* the time. She was always snapping pictures at the worst possible moment and from the worst possible angle. Douglas burned all of mine."

"Douglas was your husband?"

"I know what you're thinking, but we were separated at the time. That was years later, when he burned all my photos. At the time, he couldn't have cared less."

"That's hard to believe."

Joey gave that raucous seagull laugh. "Are you flirting with me?"

Ellery smiled weakly. No, he sure was not. He was just going by his own observations of human nature. Namely, people were often still jealous of their exes, sometimes even when they were the ones who initiated the breakup.

"It's the truth, though. Back then, Dougie didn't give a damn about anything but the ponies. Not me. Not even his kid. Nowadays, we'd say, *Oooh, he's struggling with addiction*. Back then...well, who cares what you call it? The jerk spent all his spare time—and spare change—at the race track. Who could live with that?"

"That would be tough," Ellery admitted. "That's why you left him?"

"That's right." She sounded defiant as if she thought Ellery might judge her, but no way. He couldn't even imagine what life with a compulsive gambler would be like. Add a child into the mix, and he didn't blame her for walking out.

"What race track?" he asked. "I didn't realize there were any race tracks around here."

"Gansett. Narragansett Park. He'd take the ferry and spend the day. Sometimes he'd spend the night. I warned him again and again: s*hape up or ship out*. I even told him I'd take the kid with me. He didn't care. I bet he wouldn't even have noticed until he woke up from one of his benders and I wasn't there to fix his breakfast."

"When did you separate?"

She said vaguely, "I can't recall exactly. It was off and on. I'd have done it too, I'd have left him for good if Vern hadn't…" Her expression was hard to interpret. All the liveliness seemed to fade away, leaving her blank. She blinked tiredly, as though she'd just woken from a nap.

"That's the mystery, isn't it?" Ellery watched her carefully. "What do you think happened to Vernon?"

"He didn't run off with the po-faced peacenik, that's for sure!"

"The who? The what?"

"Eudora Page. You won't know her. The b-i-t-c-h is pushing daisies in the family plot at Seal Point." She gave an evil laugh. "I won that one!"

Was it silly to be offended on behalf of his po-faced peacenik auntie when they'd never even met?

"Right. Eudora Page was another girlfriend?"

Joey shrugged. "Not really. They grew up together, so he put up with her. If there *was* anything between them, it was kid stuff. I asked Vernon, and he always said it was nothing." Her smile was cynical. "Of course, he'd have said that either way."

"Probably."

She laughed and smacked Ellery's hand. "You men. You're all alike. Dogs."

"*Wellllll*," Ellery murmured.

Joey laughed again. "Anyway, I always figured it was a diving accident that did for Vern. Every time he and Tony got leave, they were out there on the water, hunting for shipwrecks. It makes sense that if something went wrong and Vern couldn't get out, they'd hush it up. The Shandys,

I mean." She nodded knowingly. "They wouldn't want any cops involved."

No doubt true.

"So Tony Bernard was on the island when Vernon went missing?"

"Yep. He sure was."

"Was there any trouble between them?"

She frowned. "I don't think so. Thick as thieves, those two. You know he was engaged to Vera? Tony. He was engaged to Vera. He was crazy about that b-i—"

"Yep," Ellery broke in. "What happened there? They seemed to have a very long engagement. Was that usual for the times?"

"I used to wonder about that too. He was nuts about Vera. And she was nuts about him. Maybe he didn't want to make her a widow. Which is what he would have done, it turns out."

"I saw his obituary. That must have been tough."

She shrugged her bony shoulders. "Life can't always be a barrel of laughs. You'll find out soon enough. *I'd* have married him when I had the chance, if I were her. She cried her eyes out when he died. But maybe deep down she blamed Tony for letting Vern get drowned."

"Is that a possibility?" Vera hadn't even hinted at such a scenario. But she *had* put Tony's name on that list as a possible suspect.

"No way. They were buddies. Navy buddies. That's a special bond. There's a code of honor. Right?"

"I guess so. But people don't always do the honorable thing. Sometimes they panic. Sometimes they don't realize there's a problem until it's too late." Ellery suggested delicately, "Especially if there's treasure involved?"

That weird blank look came over Joey's face again. She didn't respond. Didn't even look at him. She stared out the French doors at the pseudo-tropical garden of white hibiscus and pink calycanthus.

She said dreamily, "Back then, we had great music. Not like now. We all used to listen to the Beach Boys and Dick Dale and the Del Tones. Not Vernon. He said that was kid stuff. He liked the Mills Brothers!" Her smile twisted. "There was a jukebox in the Deep Dive, and every time one of those Mills Brothers' songs came on, he'd look over at her...and she'd look over at him."

After a moment, Ellery asked, "Can you tell me what you remember about that day, Joey?"

He couldn't read the look she shot him. She shook her head. "Nothing. Because I don't know what day it was. I know Vera reported him missing on the Monday, but nobody took it seriously. Or, I guess, the Navy took it seriously, but they thought he'd gone AWOL. Which he'd *never* have done."

"Vera seems to think it was Thursday."

"I didn't work that night." Joey smiled. "That's a funny thing to remember after all this time. I pulled that shift for a lot of years, though, so maybe it's not so funny." She shrugged. "I wasn't there."

Someone knocked softly on the half-open door, then pushed the door wide. A large, frizzy-haired woman in peach-colored scrubs and rose-tinted glasses said, "May I have a word with you, Mr. Parker?"

"Sure." Ellery rose.

"Send him right back!" Joey called. "I want to keep him for a pet."

The large woman laughed merrily and glared at Ellery.

Uh-oh.

Ellery stepped into the gleaming hallway, which reeked of that distressing disinfectant-meets-plastic-tropical-flower fragrance.

"I'm Frances Crane, the director of Sunset Shores. I'm afraid I'm going to have to ask you to leave, *Mr. Parker*."

The emphasis on *Mr. Parker* left Ellery in no doubt that Ms. Crane knew he was using an alias. Which, from her perspective, probably seemed a little sinister.

He tried to explain. "Honestly, I don't mean Mrs. Franklin any harm. We're just chatting."

Ms. Crane snapped, "Mrs. Franklin is not well enough to receive visitors."

"She's not? She seems okay. I wasn—"

"*Oh?* And are you now also a doctor in addition to being an author and movie star?"

Ouch. Worse than he'd thought.

"I'm definitely not a movie star," Ellery protested. "Look, Ms. Crane—"

"No, *you* look. And it's *Mrs.* Crane."

"Mrs. Crane, I think we've started off on the wrong foot."

"If you're referring to your *lying* to my staff and patient, then yes, we've most definitely started off on the wrong foot."

"I apologize for using my pen name. I did check in at the front desk. It's not like I sneaked in here in the dead of night."

"The front desk made a mistake in agreeing to your request. Mrs. Franklin is not well enough for visitors."

"Mrs. Franklin *invited* me to visit."

"Mrs. Franklin is not well enough for visitors," Mrs. Crane repeated in an I-could-do-this-all-day tone of voice.

"All visitors or just me?"

Mrs. Crane smiled tightly. "Will you leave voluntarily, or must I phone the police?"

Two thoughts occurred to Ellery. First, he was not going to win this battle. In fact, with every word out of his mouth, he was probably making matters worse. Second, he really, *really* did not want Jack receiving a phone call that his boyfriend was harassing old ladies in nursing homes.

Ellery replied straight off Kingston's script. "Again, I apologize for overstepping. Good afternoon." If he'd had a bowler hat, he'd have doffed it to her. As it was, he merely skedaddled.

CHAPTER ELEVEN

Tackle Shandy was sitting on the front steps when Ellery arrived home that evening. A large white box rested on the pavement beside him.

"Just what I need," Ellery muttered to his copilot.

It had been a long day. A busy day and, from a sleuthing, if not bookselling perspective, a good day, but long. After he'd locked up at the Crow's Nest, he'd gone grocery-shopping to pick up everything he needed to make Jack a really terrific supper. It was going to be a long night too, which he looked forward too, naturally, but he *was* tired. He didn't have the patience or energy for another run-in with anyone, let alone a gorilla like Tackle. And he couldn't imagine any other purpose of a visit from Tackle.

Ellery parked and got out, leaving Watson safely inside the vehicle—a consideration Watson did not AT ALL appreciate, judging by the increasingly outraged tenor of the yips and cries that followed Ellery across the drive.

"Can I help you?" he called.

"You installed a security system." Tackle grinned hugely at what he imagined was a private joke.

Ellery reached the bottom of the steps. "That's right."

A muffled *Arf! Arf! Arf!* drifted on the evening breeze.

"It's a good one. Must have cost you plenty."

"It wasn't cheap."

"But I guess you're not worrying about money anymore." Tackle thrust his chin in the general direction of the yellow and coral roses and the sparkling white gravel. "You got all Brandon Abbott's money. *Conveniently.*"

Ellery gave a disbelieving laugh. "What are you suggesting? There's no mystery about who killed Brandon. As for money, authors don't make as much money as you seem to think."

Arf! Arf! Arf!

"They make more than you do running that bookstore." It was hard to argue with that. Brandon had certainly made more money writing books than Ellery did selling them. Not, however, as much as Ellery had made acting. That was because Ellery had a very good agent, and Brandon's business manager appeared to have been either incompetent or crooked.

None of which he was going to get into with Tackle Shandy, Esquire.

ARF! ARF! ARF!

Watson's barking was getting louder and louder with each passing minute. Hopefully, he would not start hurling himself at the VW's windows.

"Is there some reason for this visit?" Ellery inquired. "I mean, I always enjoy it when you drop in, but..."

Tackle didn't miss Ellery's innuendo, but he also wasn't bothered by it. His eyes glinted with malicious mirth. He patted the lid of the box beside him.

"Gram sent you a bunch of old photos and postcards and papers. She thinks they might help you do whatever you're supposed to be doing."

"Thanks. That's great." That was an unlooked-for assist. Despite sending him on this quest, Vera had been oddly reticent to supply him with anything but the most bare bones information. Ellery interpreted that to mean she wanted answers but was afraid of what those answers might be.

"These are family heirlooms, so if anything happens to them, it's on you."

"I'll take good care of them." Ellery reached for the box.

Tackle's hand slammed down like an anvil falling from the sky. "I hope so for your sake. Now, so *we're* clear, you're not to *open* this box."

Ellery straightened. "Huh?"

"You're not to go through or even look at these photos. You're not to ask any more questions or talk to any more people about my family. Do you understand?"

"Not really. No."

"You take a week, two weeks, whatever you think will be convincing, and then you tell Gram you tried everything you could think of, but you couldn't come up with anything on what happened to Vernon."

"You want me to lie to your grandmother?"

Tackle avoided going on the record with that one. "Vernon is dead and buried, and you digging into other people's dirt isn't going to change that."

"Are you sure?"

"What's that mean?"

"Are you sure he's buried? I thought the popular theory was he had a fatal accident while diving for treasure."

Tackle jumped to his feet, and Ellery was pretty sure he was going to punch him, although he wasn't exactly sure why. Was the word *treasure* a hot button? Why? It wasn't like that was a new theory.

Then he got it.

The Shandys suspected each other of possible involvement.

Or rather, Vera, suspected her family of possible involvement.

Either way, Ellery recognized that glittery fury in Tackle's eyes and the clenching and unclenching of his ham-sized hands. He braced himself, trying to remember all those hand-to-hand combat techniques he'd learned from Danny Boyega, who'd coordinated the fight scenes in the *Happy Halloween! You're Dead* films, but was unable to think of anything—except how much it hurt to get punched by accident. Never mind how it would feel to get punched on purpose.

He swallowed, remembering that Tackle had gone to prison for manslaughter. Maybe Tackle remembered that too because the glitter in his eyes faded.

"Wherever he is, it's none of your business, and Gram should have remembered that before she started airing our dirty laundry. If you know what's good for you, you'll leave this alone."

Ellery put his hands up. "Okay."

Tackle eyed him narrowly. "Okay?"

"Was that the wrong answer?"

"It's the right answer. I don't believe you."

"I don't know what to tell you."

"I want you to agree to leave this alone. I want you to stop looking into what happened to Vernon."

"And I said okay."

Vernon seemed baffled. "Stop saying that!" Ellery spread his hand—which seemed to bewilder Tackle all the more. "Are you crazy? What the hell is the matter with you?"

"I don't know what you want from me. Your grandmother is never going to believe I couldn't find out *anything*. I'm a terrible liar, so when she asks me what's going on, I'm going to end up telling her the truth. And even if I stop poking around, it's too late to quash an investigation."

"It's not too late!"

Ellery couldn't hide his impatience. "Of *course* it's too late. The coins are with RIMAP, which means ultimately there will be marine archeologists all over this place, looking for the rest of the treasure."

Tackle's lips parted.

"I have no control over that. None. Nada. Zilch. You have no control over that. It's a done deal."

"It's not—"

"Secondly, I've already talked to Police Chief Carson about this, so he's bound to take another look at the case. It doesn't matter what I do or don't do. The investigation is happening with or without me. You can threaten me from now till the end of time. You're not stopping anything." Ellery added hastily, "Except me, of course."

"I'm not *threatening* you. I'm giving you a piece of friendly advice."

"I'm getting a lot of that lately."

Tackle suddenly looked shaken, as if another much worse thought had dawned on him. He stared at Ellery, but clearly, he saw something else, something that scared the heck out of him.

Which, you would think, would take a lot.

"I'm just being honest," Ellery said. "I'm sorry."

Tackle seemed to snap back to the present. He glowered at Ellery. "Not one word to my gram. You got that?"

"Yes."

"Don't be a smartass."

Ellery sighed.

Tackle hesitated. Maybe he felt a more formal end to the scene was required. He opted for pointing his finger pistol-like at Ellery's forehead and quoting, "'Dead men tell no tales.'"

Nice. One of the classics.

Tackle laughed at Ellery's glare, turned without haste and sauntered down the steps.

As he walked past Ellery's VW, he tapped the passenger window, driving Watson to still greater fury.

ARF! ARF! ARF!

Tackle laughed and kept walking. Ellery watched him climb into his battered Ford pickup, roar the engine a few times, and then deliberately screech around the halfmoon drive, kicking up gravel and dirt, before tearing off down the road.

"You ass." Ellery watched Tackle's taillights fade into the twilight.

When he was sure Tackle was done for the evening, he went to the VW and let Watson, who was beside himself by that point, out of the car.

"I'm sorry, buddy. But I don't trust that guy." It was only too easy to picture Tackle giving a yappy little dog a hard, swift kick into the afterlife.

Watson leaped into Ellery's arms, whining and licking his chin.

"I know, I know." Ellery kissed the top of his head. "You would have been a big help. This was no reflection on you and your security team. You run a very tight ship."

It seemed Watson had finished lodging his formal protest because he began to wiggle to be let down. He sprang away, racing up the driveway, barking at approaching headlights.

Ellery felt a flare of alarm, but the next moment he recognized the muted *hum* of Jack's SUV. He whistled to Watson, lest, in the fading light, he be run over by his hero, and Watson raced back, running in circles around Ellery.

"Yep. I see him," Ellery murmured.

Jack pulled up beside Ellery's VW. The SUV's headlights flicked off, the radio fell silent, the engine died. Jack got out, greeting Watson, who proceeded to explain recent events at the top of his lungs.

Ellery went to meet Jack.

Jack kissed him hello, but it was on automatic pilot. "Was that Tackle Shandy?"

"Mm-hm. He was trying to warn me off the case."

Jack's expression was a study, and Ellery laughed. "It's okay. It was mostly bluster."

Jack didn't look reassured. "Don't make the mistake of thinking he's all bluster and no beef."

"Pardon me?"

"You know what I mean. Shandy's got poor impulse control and the brainpower of a minnow. Don't forget, this is someone who did prison time for manslaughter."

"I'm not forgetting. It's not my first run-in with Tackle."

"Exactly. And with that kind of guy, familiarity breeds contempt."

"To tell you the truth, I think Tackle was upset because he just realized his father committed murder fifty-nine years ago."

Jack stared. "You're telling me, you think Rocky Shandy killed his cousin Vernon?"

"I think Tackle thinks so. And I think Vera is afraid it's so. I don't know. It's possible in that Rocky is one of the few people at that time who could have known that Vernon had found gold doubloons. And he doesn't sound like the most upstanding of citizens."

"No," Jack said slowly.

"But also, it seems like if Rocky or another family member killed Vernon, the rest of the family would have figured it out by now."

"Maybe." Jack seemed unconvinced of that.

"And, would Rocky be dumb enough to kill Vernon without actually having the coins in his possession?"

Jack made a nix-that-idea noise. "This is entirely speculation. You have no idea under what circumstances such a crime would have occurred. It might have nothing to do with pirate's gold. It could have been two family members falling out over something completely unrelated."

"Okay, true." Ellery grimaced. "Anyway, I hate to tell you, but dinner's going to be late. I just got here myself. The groceries are still in the car."

Jack slid his arm around Ellery's waist, pulling him in for a quick hug. "No worries. I'm just glad to be here. We've got all night, plus we've both got tomorrow off, so I don't care if we eat at midnight."

They started across the drive, Watson trotting ahead.

"What's that box?" Jack asked.

"Vera sent over some photos—" Ellery stopped in his tracks, staring up at the shining window on the second floor.

CHAPTER TWELVE

"**D**id you plug that lamp back in?" Jack asked.

"I sure didn't."

"Okay, that's weird." Jack let go of Ellery and strode up the steps. Using his key, he unlocked the door and entered the house, Ellery on his heels.

"Maybe it's battery operated." Even as Ellery said it, he knew that couldn't be right. The lamp was too old to be battery operated. A short in the wiring made sense. Though not if the lamp was still unplugged.

"Maybe." Jack was already across the front hall and heading up the staircase. Ellery and Watson followed.

The hall on the second story was dark, so there went one theory.

"Was the contractor here today?" Jack asked.

"No. Nobody's working here on the weekends."

Even before they got to the doorway of the small room, Ellery knew the lamp was not on. No light spilled through to the hall. The room was dark.

Jack paused in the doorway, feeling for a light switch. "Is there another lamp? An overhead light?"

"No." That now-familiar sense of unease crawled over Ellery. "There's just the rocking chair, the table, the lamp, and some empty bookshelves."

Jack suddenly laughed. "I think I know the answer to this mystery. We saw the setting sun reflecting off the windowpanes."

"Right! Of course!" Ellery laughed too and relaxed. However, he couldn't help asking, "But why just that window?"

"The angle of the house. The angle of the sun. You weren't here this time last year, so for all you know, that window glows all autumn long."

"That makes sense." Did it, though? Ellery's relief at a simple explanation was already receding. Sure, there had to be a simple explanation, but maybe this was too simple. Wouldn't he and Jack have noticed if the sunset had been reflected in the window? That light had sure looked like it was shining from within the house.

But what were the other alternatives?

"So, no ghost?" he joked.

"No ghost." Jack was joking too, and yet Ellery could tell by his tone that the idea had also crossed his mind. Well, Jack had grown up reading the Hardy Boys and Encyclopedia Brown and The Three Investigators. It would be odd if the thought *hadn't* occurred to him. The closest Ellery had come was in college, watching Saturday morning episodes of *Scooby-Doo* with Brandon while recovering from Friday night hangovers.

He glanced around for Watson and saw him sitting a couple of yards down the hall. Watson's ears were uncharacteristically pinned back, and he looked small and defensive. He whined when Ellery looked at him, as though they were on opposite sides of a chasm.

"Does that room feel cold to you?" Ellery asked Jack.

Jack snorted. "This whole house feels cold to me." He closed the door to the room.

Hadn't they done that before? How had that door opened?

Stop. The entire house *was* cold this time of year. And with all the work being done on the ancient wiring, it was more than possible that the hall light was flickering on and off. Ellery had enough mysteries to keep him occupied without looking for new ones. Especially if the new ones were going to make him nervous about staying in his home alone at night.

Jack glanced at him, said briskly, "What do you say we go downstairs, have a drink, and I'll help you make dinner."

And *that* was the scariest thing that had happened all day.

It felt too chilly and damp to barbecue, so Ellery decide to pan-fry the steaks.

He and Jack carried in the groceries, and while Jack went to get something out of his SUV, Ellery poured a glass of wine and fed Watson, who seemed back to his normal cheery little self.

Jack returned carrying a manila folder, which he handed to Ellery.

"In lieu of a bottle of wine, I brought you this. Just...it's for your eyes only. You can share the information, such as it is, but not the file itself. Understand?"

"Yes." Ellery took the folder. "What is this?"

"Vernon Shandy's case file."

Ellery's jaw dropped. "Are you allowed to do that?"

Jack gave a half-laugh. "I'm glad that's a consideration for you. Yes. This isn't the original file. I'm sharing a copy with you because the Shandy family wants someone to take another look at the case and you're their designated representative. I'm extending you the same courtesy I would any investigator working at the behest of the victim's family."

Ellery was only partly joking when he said, "That feels like a whole lot of pressure."

"Good. It should. This is serious stuff." Jack's smile was wry. "Also, I read through the case notes while I was trying to decide whether to let you have the file, and having a fresh pair of eyes to go over everything isn't a bad idea."

Ellery opened the file, glanced over the single printed page and a handful of loose notes. "What everything? Is this it?"

"That's it. The missing person's report Vera filed after Vernon disappeared, and the handwritten notes of an un-named detective made, apparently, while chatting on the phone."

"It's not much."

Jack's sigh was weary. "No. It sure isn't. It looks like Vera was right about one thing. No one took her concerns seriously."

"Do you think there was any kind of follow-up beyond a couple of phone calls?"

"It doesn't look like it."

By now, Ellery knew Jack well enough to read the dis-gust and disapproval in his eyes. If there was one thing Jack hated, it was sloppy police work.

"Was it because Vernon was a Shandy? Or did they just assume he'd be back in a few days?"

"Probably a combination of things. If you look at the date, Vernon is supposed to have gone missing the night of the Fourth of July. The island would have been packed with people partying. The department would already have been strained to capacity over what would have ended up being a long holiday weekend. Vernon was in the Navy, a grown man known to be more than capable of taking care of himself. I think the tendency, even today, would be to give it some time, see if he showed up over the next few days."

"I can see that."

"The situation would be further complicated by the fact that he was due back at Naval Station Newport on that following Tuesday. It wasn't unreasonable to think he might have left early and not bothered to tell anyone."

"But he never returned to base."

"No."

"Who takes jurisdiction in that situation? The military police?" Ellery asked.

"If enlisted personnel go missing off installation, usually military and civilian law enforcement try to coordinate. In this case, it looks like PICO PD left it up to the Navy, and the Navy drew their own conclusions."

Ellery gazed down at those brief, scribbled notations on faded paper. "It must have been pretty awful for Vernon's family."

Jack nodded. "Yes."

While Ellery preheated the oven for the twice-baked potatoes and drizzled oil over a frying pan, Jack poured himself a short Scotch.

That was unusual. Jack rarely drank spirits. He preferred beer and occasionally wine, though Ellery knew he did enjoy Scotch. Ellery's bottle of The Macallan Double Cask 12 Old had barely been touched during the months he and Jack had been dating.

"How was your day?" Ellery asked, popping the potatoes in the oven.

"A day I don't hear from anyone on the town council is a good day," Jack replied.

Ellery smiled to himself as he sautéed the steaks and fried the bacon for the twice-baked potatoes. Jack was ex-

tremely good at dealing with the different (difficult) per-
sonalities of the town council, but it was probably his least
favorite part of his job. He listened absently as Jack talked
out the minor irritations and frustrations of his day.

After five minutes, he flipped the steaks, reduced the
heat to medium, and set about melting butter in a small pan
for the red-wine mushroom sauce.

"Did you want another glass of wine?"

"Thanks." Ellery checked the steaks, added mushrooms
and shallots to the saucepan, checked the potatoes.

Jack refilled Ellery's glass. "How did your sleuthing go?"

Ellery filled him in on the visit to Sunset Shores, and
Jack listened, but seemed to have little to say other than a
quiet, "Uh-oh," when Ellery explained about his encounter
with Mrs. Crane.

"I know. Maybe she's not supposed to have visitors, but
the staff didn't seem to think twice about letting me in."

"Do me a favor and don't—"

"No, no," Ellery promised. "I know how awkward it
would be to have to arrest me."

"You have no idea."

Ellery sipped his wine and considered. "Joey said something I found interesting, though. I asked her what she remembered about the day Vernon disappeared."

"What did she say?"

"She said she didn't remember what day it was. That no
one knew for sure what day it was."

Jack started to answer, but Ellery said quickly, "That
seems unlikely. That she wouldn't remember. But that's not
the interesting part."

"Okay. What's the interesting part?"

"I told her Vera believed Vernon went missing on Thursday, and Joey said, *I didn't work that night.*"

Jack was silent. Then he said slowly, "You didn't mention the Deep Dive?"

"No. In fact, I don't think I even specified *night.*"

"*Ah.*" Jack nodded. "Okay. Yes. You're right. That's interesting. Why did she assume Vernon going missing had anything to do with the Deep Dive?"

"Right? That's what I thought."

The timer dinged, Ellery put his glass down and returned to the fray.

They continued to chat as the steaks rested, the bacon drained, and Ellery made the buttermilk Dijon dressing for the chopped salad, but their conversation revolved around non-lethal topics like wainscotting, ceiling medallions, the best flowers for autumn planting, and whether Nan Sweeny could beat George Lansing if she did decide to run for mayor in the spring.

Ellery mentioned his plan to invite some of his old friends for a house party in November, and Jack raised his brows, but said only, "That should be fun," in a noncommittal tone that probably meant he'd figure out a way to be attending a conference on the mainland that weekend.

When the meal was at last prepared, Ellery said, "I think it's finally too cold to eat on the terrace. You want to eat in here?"

Surprisingly, Jack said, "We could try out those new chandeliers and eat in the dining room."

Ellery smiled. "Well, in that case, we'll use the good china."

"You keep raising the bar," Jack murmured when they had finished their meals and Ellery served Jack's favorite mocha-pecan ice-cream bonbons.

Ellery was amused. He put the comment down to the fact that Jack was on his third Scotch. Ellery too was drinking more than usual. Not that either of them was drunk, but they were definitely relaxed. Ellery couldn't help wondering if that was by design. There was something going on with Jack, some undercurrent he didn't quite understand.

He smiled, ate his dessert, watched Jack gravely eat his bonbons.

Jack's handsome face in the gentle light of the new chandeliers was serious, even preoccupied. His dark lashes threw crescents on his cheekbones. The corner of his mouth was slightly downturned and pensive. Ellery felt a flicker of worry. What was going on with Jack?

Jack raised his lashes, met Ellery's gaze, and said with what seemed to be total sincerity, "Have I ever told you you're the perfect boyfriend?"

Okay. Jack *had* drunk too much. Clearly.

Ellery laughed. "Definitely not! I'd have remembered that."

Jack looked taken aback. "Okay, maybe not perfect, but I had to have told you how much I..." Jack cleared his throat.

"Appreciate a home-cooked meal?" teased Ellery.

Jack insisted, "Appreciate *you*."

Ellery's face warmed. "Aww." He gave Jack a quick, uncertain smile. "Thanks. Thank you, Jack."

Jack was affectionate and complimentary, but he wasn't prone to what Nora would call *romanceifying*. This was probably one of the most blatantly flattering things he'd ever said to Ellery.

"I mean it." Jack sounded sincere. He studied Ellery's expression, seemed to hesitate, and then said, "You want to go for a walk?"

Ellery smiled. "A walk in the moonlight? I would. That sounds really nice."

It was a little more complicated than during the summer months when it was still light at eight thirty, but they bundled up, grabbed flashlights, and set off, Watson scampering ahead as they walked across the meadow, holding hands.

That was a first. A really nice first. Ellery was trying to remember the last time he'd held hands with a guy—but really, he didn't want to think of any guy but Jack.

And Jack? Jack seemed lost in thought.

The countryside was always quiet, but in the autumn the quiet had a different quality. This time of year, most of the second homes and vacation cottages were empty. No distant lights twinkled from far across the fields, no woodsmoke threaded through the clouds. The only sounds were Watson crashing through brush, the pound of their feet on the damp earth, and the distant crash of waves—louder in the evening stillness.

The moon was so large and so bright, their flashlights weren't even necessary. The entire world seemed bathed in silvery light.

They walked for a minute or two without speaking, and then Ellery remembered he still hadn't told Jack about Ronny's phone call.

"Oh my gosh. I meant to tell you. My agent called yesterday."

"About the new screenplay?"

"Oh. No. Come to think of it, she didn't even mention that." Ellery brooded for a moment or two.

Jack prodded, "Your agent called…?"

"I've been offered a role in the reboot of the next *Happy Halloween! You're Dead* films."

Jack seemed to check midstride. "You're kidding."

"No."

Jack's eyes looked black in the hard moonlight. "I thought the series was finished."

"Me too. Along with my career." There was no answering smile from Jack. Ellery said, less cheerfully, "This is a reboot. I wouldn't be the star. I'm playing the same character, I guess, but now the series is about *his* son, Noah Parker Junior."

"Oh." Jack started walking again.

Not like Ellery was expecting…well, the truth was, he had no idea what to expect from Jack. He was still working out his own feelings about the unexpected opportunity to return to filmmaking. But he couldn't help feeling like Jack's reaction was especially lukewarm. Most people would see this as maybe-sort-of-kind-of a coup of sorts.

Then again, Jack would be the first to admit he knew nothing about the movie industry—and he cared even less.

"The money is—would be—really good."

"I see."

They were still holding hands, but somehow it felt like they had moved apart. Ellery gently squeezed Jack's hand, which suddenly seemed less warm and less welcoming. "You seem …like maybe you don't like the idea."

Jack glanced over, and his expression in the moonlight was hard to read. "Do *you* like the idea? I thought you were finished with acting. Or at least with making movies."

"I am. This would be a one-time—well, I guess a three-time—deal."

"*Three* times?"

"It's a three-film deal."

Crickets. Well, not literally. It was too cold for crickets. But yeah. Crickets.

"I...well, that's great."

It was so obviously *not* great in Jack's view that, in another time and place, it would have been funny.

"But if you don't like the idea..."

Okay. Really? Was he really going to turn down the opportunity, that money, solely because Jack didn't like the idea? It's not like he and Jack were—

Right on cue, if a little crushingly, Jack said, "It's not up to me. It's none of my business."

"No. Right. Well." Ellery let go of Jack's hand and walked a few steps ahead. He shrugged because he was abruptly out of anything to say. And if he didn't pull himself together, he was going to trip over Watson or something equally embarrassing.

There was really no reason to be so hurt. Jack was right. This was Ellery's decision. It felt important to Ellery to get Jack's thoughts—he had a pretty good idea of those now—but it was clearly not important to Jack that Ellery have his input. Ellery was on his own in this—as he was always alone.

Because that was the truth. Yes, he and Jack had a nice, companionable, affectionate (occasionally it even felt loving) relationship. But Jack showed no signs of wanting anything more. Ellery was happy enough with the status quo. Mostly. He'd certainly thought so three and a half minutes ago.

The whole situation made him mad—at himself, yes, but also a bit at Jack, who really could be kind of a jerk sometimes—but mostly at himself for being so *stupid* and emotional—

"No," Jack said, and caught him up, taking Ellery's hand and drawing him to a stop. "Ellery, I didn't mean... I don't know what to say. But yes, it's your decision, but also yes, of course it's my business. We're…"

Ellery waited, but it seemed that Jack still didn't know what to say.

But he was trying. "Would you be on location somewhere? Would you be traveling a lot? Are you thinking of closing the bookshop? Of leaving Pirate's Cove?"

"No. What? NO."

"I'm not sure how to feel about this because I don't know what it means." Jack's gaze was dark and earnest, his voice troubled. "My gut feeling? If I'm honest, I don't like the idea. Partly because I don't know what this means for us." He offered a tentative smile. "I guess I'm one of those boring stick-in-the-muds who doesn't like change."

"I don't know what it means either," Ellery admitted. He wiped his wrist against his eyes.

Jack groaned, pulled him close, kissed his wet eyelids, the side of his nose, the corner of his mouth. "Ell, don't. I'm sorry. If this is what you want, I'm glad for you. And more money…that house eats money like Cookie Monster gobbles sugar cookies. More money is always going to come in handy."

"I don't know if it's what I want," Ellery said. "I turned the part down at first, but then Ronny started quoting numbers, and it's a lot of dough."

"But you've got Brandon's…what do you call it? Literary estate."

"Yes. But that really nice payout I got last month was largely due to this movie deal. Brandon's book sales went sky high after he died, but that's not going to last forever. His publisher will repackage things and put out new audio and collections, but the demand for his work isn't—he wasn't a writer for the ages. In fairness, he didn't want to be."

"Okay. Well."

"It would just be nice to have something for a rainy day again. To rebuild my savings. And if I turn this down, I'm not likely to get another chance. I'll be closing that door for good."

"But if you accept, does it end there? Will there be more movies?"

"I don't think so. I don't know. But the thing is, I don't want to go back into acting. I love my life. I've never been happier than I am now." He wiped his nose. "Well, maybe not at this minute, but the last few months. I do want the money, though. And it would be kind of fun to make a movie that actually has a budget and top players. The role probably won't be very demanding. It could be a couple of days, maybe one day, and I'd be out of there."

"Or not."

Ellery sighed. "Or not."

Jack nodded, but that seemed to be more at his own thoughts. He said wryly, "I have to admit, I didn't see this coming."

"Me neither."

"But whatever you decide, I support your decision."

"Thanks."

"And…if you do decide to make another movie, or three, it won't change anything between us."

Ellery nodded. When Jack pulled him in again, he wrapped his arms around Jack's shoulders and kissed him long and hard, kissed him with all his heart.

He knew Jack sincerely meant every word. He just wished Jack sounded more convinced of what he was saying.

And he wished *he* felt more convinced of what Jack was saying.

CHAPTER THIRTEEN

Barring the rare police emergency, Ellery and Jack spent most Sundays together.

Before the professional renovations at Captain's Seat had started, they either went diving or worked on the house, but it was starting to get chilly for water sports, so that Sunday afternoon they hiked out to the site where the original Deep Dive once stood overlooking the white-capped waters of Old Harbor.

"I didn't realize there would be so little of the building left." Ellery gazed down at the surprisingly small foundation of the pub. Grass and wildflowers grew through the broken stone and cement footprint. A few charred timbers lay scattered over the hillside.

"Were you hoping for a skeleton beneath the floorboards?"

"At the least. Or maybe hidden behind the bricks of a crumbling wall."

"Life is full of disappointments." Jack was kidding. But maybe not entirely?

Though maybe Jack thought that was a little heavy too, because he said, "The fire started at two thirty a.m. It was summer, a hot and dry June in 1965. The flames ripped through these old buildings like tinder."

"Where did the fire start?"

"The Hotel Royale." Jack's mouth curved in a humorless smile. "There were rumors of arson. Rumors the hotel was torched for the insurance."

"Was it?"

Jack shrugged. "It's possible. But the hotel was built in 1915. It was in seriously bad shape by then, so it's also possible that it really was just a grease fire."

"A grease fire at two thirty in the morning?"

"By that time, rooms at the Royale were being rented out as cheap housing, so yeah. You had all kinds of safety-code violations going on."

"Ah." Normally, Ellery would have teased Jack about his preoccupation with health and safety protocols, but not today. Jack had been a little... Not distant, but just a bit reserved that morning. It was nothing Ellery could put his finger on. Jack had been funny and affectionate—his normal Sunday morning self—yet there was something.

"Was anyone killed?"

"No," Jack said. "Miraculously, nobody died in that fire. That was the good news. The bad news was everyone on this side of the harbor lost their homes and businesses. Even the businesses that weren't burned, they couldn't survive as isolated shops. The old pier burned down too."

"Where the heck was the fire department?"

Jack gave him a cynical smile. "That was the question of the hour, and one reason the rumors started. Coincidentally, another mysterious fire had been set on the other end of the village. Pirate's Cove's fire department was already busy when this fire broke out. A lot of valuable time was lost in getting over here."

"That does sound suspicious."

"Coincidences happen, but yeah. It sure does." Jack shaded his eyes, gazing out across the windswept fields and choppy blue water. His profile looked bleak.

Ellery regarded him for a moment, then turned back to the ruins of the Deep Dive.

He was a little disappointed. Not that he had really expected to uncover Vernon's grave in the cellar of the old ruins, but he'd hoped to gain some insight by visiting what had surely been the scene of the crime.

Vernon had disappeared in 1963, so the fire two years later was unlikely to have had any connection.

"This must have been a very old building at the time it burned."

"One of the oldest on the island. It was originally the Shandy home."

"Their *home*? Hm. One of the oldest structures, and they later turned it into a pub. What do you want to bet, the original Deep Dive was connected to the tunnels?"

The founding fathers of Pirate's Cove had built an elaborate network of tunnels beneath the village. Whether the original purpose had been defense fortifications or smuggling or both, local families had continued adding and closing branches right through Prohibition. Accordingly, no accurate map of the entire system existed. In fact, no one living had ever explored the entire complex.

Jack smiled faintly. "I wouldn't take that bet. There's no doubt they had an entrance to the tunnels. I'm sure there's an entrance to the tunnels in the current Deep Dive."

"Did anyone check the tunnels for Vernon?"

"No one from PICO PD, I'm guessing." Jack was definitely not happy about the failings of his predecessors. "But I'd be pretty damned amazed if the Shandys didn't move heaven and earth trying to find him."

Ellery agreed. It was difficult to imagine Vera taking no for an answer in any circumstances, let alone when she feared for the safety of someone she loved.

"I'll verify that with her, but I agree."

"Did you want to walk over to the village and grab a late lunch? Or did you want to drive back to the house? Or would you like to do something else?"

"Let's grab some lunch." It was a beautiful, brisk day, and the walk would be good exercise.

Jack whistled for Watson, and the three of them started down the weathered paved road.

In the translucent afternoon light, the hillside, covered in shadbush and chokecherry, seemed to glow with sunset shades of copper, crimson, and cream. Vines of Virginia creeper and poison ivy laced the silvery stones of crumbling walls. Seabirds soared and swooped overhead, jeering at Watson's attempts to chase them down.

Ellery said, "I don't know why Vera gave me so little information to start with. It's like she wanted me to investigate, but she *didn't* want me to investigate."

"At a guess, I'd say she's afraid a family member is involved. I think that's why she stopped pestering the authorities. She wants to know the truth, but she doesn't want to give you evidence that could eventually be used against someone she cares about in an official investigation."

"That's a pretty fine line."

"Vera's been walking pretty fine lines all her life. Watch this patch. The soil is eroding."

They picked their way down to the flat stretch of road along the beach.

"Why didn't they rebuild over here?" Ellery asked. "Why did they just leave it to return to nature?"

"The hotel, which was the major draw, was gone. The pier was gone. Also, that fire would have clearly shown how vulnerable the businesses and homes on this side of the harbor were to natural disasters. I can see why people would hesitate. Especially when, back then, there was still plenty of available real estate in the village."

Ellery, still thinking over their earlier conversation, said, "If Vera believes there's any possibility of prosecution, there's only one member of her family left who could be a suspect."

"Rocky," Jack agreed.

"Right. Her uncle Barry is gone. So it would have to be Rocky she's trying to protect."

"I don't think Rocky would go to trial anyway. I don't think he'd be found competent."

"But Tackle had to have some reason to warn me off."

Jack gave him a sideways glance. "That might not be concern for Rocky. That might be concern that someone else is going to find Vernon's treasure before him."

Given the lengths Tackle had already gone to obtain the coins, Ellery couldn't argue with that. "Do we know anything more about those coins yet?"

"They're definitely doubloons, whether genuine or fake. But no. I plan on giving Dr. Shelton at RIMAP a call tomorrow." Jack added, "Like I said, Rocky might not have killed Vernon over the treasure. Brothers, cousins, whatever they were, fall out over a lot of things. Vernon was a notorious womanizer, so who knows? But the idea that his entire family wouldn't be aware he'd found those doubloons defies belief. After he was gone, the whereabouts of the coins—and possible treasure—would be of topmost concern to the Shandys."

Ellery nodded. He was watching Watson cautiously approach what appeared to be a large piece of driftwood in the road ahead.

Watson raised one paw and sniffed cautiously at the log. He backed up, dropped to his front paws, wagging his tail, and began to bark.

Arf. Arf. Arf.

"What's he playing with?"

Jack frowned. Watson pounced to one side, then the other, barking all the while. A gull sitting at the other end of the...object took flight, squawking protest.

"Jesus Christ," Jack said quietly.

"Oh *no*." Ellery turned to him. "Is that—is that a *body*?"

He was speaking to open air. Jack was already running toward the—gulp—crime scene. "*Watson,*" he roared.

That was a tone Watson had never heard from Jack before, and he backed away so quickly, he did a somersault.

"*Get out of here!*"

Watson fled toward Ellery, who arrived seconds after Jack and stopped a few feet away. Watson stood on his hind legs, pawing Ellery, and Ellery hauled him up. His gaze was riveted on the man—definitely a man—lying facedown on the cracked pavement.

Red hair...big shoulders...big everything...dressed in black splattered with...

Ellery swallowed queasily. A horrifying red-brown stain surrounded and spread from the body.

"Don't come any closer," Jack warned him.

"Is he— Who is that?"

The look Jack gave him was so stark, Ellery felt as if a winter wind swept over him. He sucked in a breath, and

Watson licked his chin. It took Ellery a moment to get enough air into his lungs to ask, "What happened to him?"

"It looks like he was hit by a tank."

Ellery closed his eyes. When he opened them, Jack was gazing at him assessingly.

"You okay?"

"Swell."

"I'll stay with the body. You hike back to my vehicle and stay there."

"Why?"

"Because you had a run-in with Tackle Shandy yesterday evening, and now he's dead in what sure as hell looks to me like homicide. I don't want anyone able to say you had access to this crime scene or could contaminate it in any way."

Ellery gaped. "Is someone liable to say that?"

Jack's look was pure exasperation. "It's not like the entire police department hasn't noticed you've been involved in A LOT of homicides since you arrived on this island."

"I'm a suspect?"

Jack bit back what he started to say, settling for a relatively mild, "We were never apart from the minute Shandy left Captain's Seat, so if you're a suspect, I am too. But for everyone's sake, go back to the SUV and wait for me."

Ellery nodded tightly. He wasn't mad at Jack. He was mad at the situation. He put Watson down, snapped his leash to his collar, and turned away.

Jack called, "Ellery?"

Ellery turned back.

"I'm sorry our day together turned out like this."

Ellery summoned a smile. "Not your fault."

"I'll meet you up there as soon as I can."

Ellery nodded again and started the walk back to Jack's SUV.

That was the end of Ellery's weekend, of course.

Granted, it was the end of Tackle's weekend too.

When the crime-scene team finally arrived, Jack returned to the SUV and told Ellery Officer Martin would drive him back to Captain's Seat.

Ellery tried to read Jack's face. "Do you know anything yet?"

Jack sighed. "I know it's going to be a long night. I'll give you a call this evening."

"If it's okay, could Martin drop me off at the Crow's Nest? I think I'd rather work than sit around wondering what's going on."

"Are you sure?"

Ellery nodded. "I'll ask Nora or Kingston to give me a ride home."

"Okay." Jack gave him a quick kiss. "Be good."

Ellery's brows drew together. "I'm not sure what that means."

"Believe me, I've noticed." But Jack was clearly teasing, and Ellery smiled feebly. Jack ruffled Watson's ears and headed back to his crime scene.

"We didn't expect to see you today, dearie," Nora greeted Ellery when he arrived at the Crow's Nest around four o'clock. She sounded ever so slightly guilty, and no wonder. The entire Silver Sleuths book club seemed to be in residence. However, since they were the only people in the store, it seemed pointless to object.

Kingston said, "We've heard the news. How are you, my boy?"

Mrs. Nelson said, "What a *terrible* experience for you!"

Which Mr. Starling waved off, saying, "He's used to it by now."

"Not really," Ellery said, stung. Jack's words about the possible suspicions of his PICO PD coworkers troubled him. Yes, from their perspective, he probably did have an unusually high rate of involvement in homicides—from *his* perspective too!

"Live by the sword, die by the sword," Mrs. Ferris said. "Tackle Shandy was no stranger to violence."

"Yes, dear, but he was a salvage diver," Nora said. "I don't suppose swords figured into it?" She looked inquiringly at Ellery.

"It looks like he was hit by a car. He was lying in the middle of the road."

"A hit and run!" Mrs. Clarence exclaimed. "I didn't see that coming!"

"Neither did Tackle," Mr. Starling retorted.

"Where?" Kingston asked.

It took Ellery a moment to understand the question. "The old road leading from where the Royale hotel used to be. Jack and I were hiking on the other side of the harbor when we found him."

There were several meaningful exchanges of glances at this information.

Ellery said quickly, "Before you ask, I don't know anything more than that. Jack had me wait in his SUV while he stayed with the body."

There were little shivers of delighted horror all around, and then Nora said, "Perhaps it's a good thing you came in today. There was a rather weird message for you on the answering machine this morning."

They all gazed at him expectantly, so he had no doubt they already knew—had discussed—what he was about to hear.

Ellery said, "Okay. I'll have a listen."

He left Watson to be petted and fussed over, went into the office, and pressed Play.

A loud and unfriendly male voice announced, "Mr. Page, this is James Franklin. Frances Crane at Sunset Shores contacted me regarding that little stunt you pulled this afternoon. What kind of man takes advantage of a sick, old woman? If you *ever* try to contact my mother again, I'm informing the police!"

The phone slammed down.

Ellery winced. Yikes. He played the message again, but there was no mistake. James Franklin's voice shook with rage as he threatened legal action. What the heck did he think Ellery had been getting up to with Mrs. Franklin? What the heck had Mrs. Crane told him?

Before this misunderstanding went any further, Ellery needed to set the record straight.

He sat down at the desk, dragged out the phone directory, turned to the earmarked page with the listing for Franklin, and punched in the numbers.

An answering machine picked up, and a factory-set female voice invited him to leave his message after the *beep.*

Ellery waited for the *beep* and said, "Mr. Franklin, this is Ellery Page. I just received your phone message, and I want to apologize—as well as explain. I'm not sure what Mrs. Crane told you, but I truly meant no offense."

There was something disconcerting about the hissing silence on the other end.

Should he leave it there? Should he keep trying to explain to the refrigerator and stove?

How old had Franklin been in 1963? It was hard to tell over the phone, but he sounded older. Not old; maybe middle-aged? Joey had referred to *the kid* a couple of times. Was that kid Franklin? Was it possible *he* had useful memories of that period?

Ellery continued, "I apologize for having used a-a nom de plume. The truth is, I'm working on a book set on the island back in the 1960s, and Vera Shandy suggested your mother might be a good source for stories about the Deep Dive and all its colorful characters."

It was easier to lie over the phone than to someone's face. However, it was going to be awkward if Franklin compared notes with his mother. Was that likely? Maybe not, if Ellery's suspicions were correct, and Mrs. Shandy was being corralled without her knowledge.

"Actually, your mother mentioned you a few times, and I'd love to interview you if you're at all willing. I promise you, there's nothing shady going on."

Ellery recited his cell phone number and hung up.

There was a chance Franklin might phone him back, but he wasn't going to hold his breath. Clearly, the guy was worried about some embarrassing information coming to light. Maybe it had to do with his father's gambling addiction, his mother's affair, or simply what sounded like a very unpleasant home life.

People tended to forget kids were around when they were talking—speaking as someone who'd picked up an awful lot of interesting backstage gossip back when he'd worn childhood's magic cloak of invisibility.

CHAPTER FOURTEEN

"**I**t's a very good sign," Mrs. Nelson was saying when Ellery returned to the book floor. "Not for poor Tackle, of course, but it means we're getting closer."

"How do you figure that?" Mr. Starling inquired. "None of *us* was run over. *He* wasn't run over." He pointed at Ellery. "It seems to me if anyone was getting close to anything, it was Tackle Shandy and the bumper of that car."

Mrs. Clarence murmured, "Oh dear. Stanley."

"Maybe so, but I don't think I'm wrong." Mr. Starling fastened his beady little gaze on Ellery. "Do *you* think I'm wrong?"

Ellery poured himself a cup of coffee from the burner on the side table beneath the portrait of the *Golden Fancy*. He was starting to feel very tired, and it wasn't only from trying to follow the Silver Sleuths' verbal ping-pong.

"I think Tackle must have known something. He definitely didn't want the case reopened. There could be a lot of reasons for that. He couldn't have any direct involvement in Vernon's disappearance, but he could've discovered the truth secondhand."

"Exactly," Nora said. "He could have *personal* involvement. Rocky could certainly be involved."

"I believe his uncle Barry was a far more likely suspect," Mrs. Nelson said.

"Barry was his grandfather, dear," Nora said.

"I mean, *Vernon's* uncle."

"*Oh!* Yes. You're quite right. Barry was Vernon's uncle, and there *was* bad blood between them."

Mrs. Ferris said abruptly, "We keep skirting the question of Eudora."

Ellery felt the weight of six pairs of eyes land on him. He raised his shoulders. "Don't worry about me. I want the truth too."

"Eudora didn't murder anyone." Nora's dismissive tone seemed to irk Mrs. Ferris.

"You can't possibly know that, Nora. Eudora was a grown woman, and you were a child. You can't pretend to have been friends with her."

"I'm not pretending anything. But I did know her a little as an adult, and I don't believe Eudora was a murderess."

Stanley said, "If she was, it was a one-time deal."

"That doesn't excuse murder, Stanley," Mrs. Ferris protested.

"She was provoked." Stanley glanced at Ellery and added, "If she did it. Which I doubt."

"She did get very odd toward the end," Mrs. Nelson mused.

"We *all* get odd toward the end," Nora retorted.

Kingston cleared his throat.

"Anyway," Mrs. Nelson said, "they were first cousins, weren't they? So I really can't see how there could have been anything between them. It's not as though this is Arkansas."

"I think you mean Kentucky," Mrs. Ferris said. "Or is it Alabama?"

Ellery said, "What are you talking about? Who was first cousins?"

"Vernon and Eudora," Mrs. Nelson answered.

"*Huh?*"

Nora said quickly, "No. They certainly were not."

"They certainly were!"

"They were *not*." Nora slanted Ellery a slightly harassed look. She shook her head. "No. Eudora's *first* cousins were Oliver, Barry, Violet, Lowell, Sidney, Everett, Virgil, and Daisy. Virgil married Dana Starling, and they had Victor, Vernon, and Vera. So, no. They were *not* first cousins."

Mrs. Clarence inquired, "What is a second cousin once removed? Can you be a first cousin once removed? Perhaps they were first cousins once removed?"

"Vernon was certainly removed," Stanley put in and gave a crazy cackle.

Nora, Mrs. Nelson, Mrs. Clarence, and Mrs. Ferris all glared at him.

"*I* didn't push the feller off a cliff," Stanley protested.

Ellery put his hands up. "STOP."

The room fell silent.

"*Who* is related to what? I mean *whom*. Am *I* closely related to the Shandys?"

"Is he closely related to the Shandys?" Mr. Starling seemed genuinely amazed. "Is he kidding?"

"There is a *slight* connection," Nora admitted.

Kingston murmured, "It's a little more than a slight connection, my dear."

My dear?

"Says the descendent of Thirza Sweeny!" exclaimed Mr. Starling.

"It was just the one time!" Nora protested.

"She founded the whole bloody line!"

"What is *happening*?" Ellery asked. Watson wagged his tail.

Kingston explained, "In the 1790s Molly Shandy married Phineas Page, and they had three children: Alec, Quillan, and Minerva."

"And so on and so forth," Nora cut in. "Really, it was a long time ago. It has no bearing on our case."

"If it was the 1790s, then I can't see how that would affect Virgil—I mean Vernon or my aunt."

Kingston opened his mouth, but Mrs. Nelson said, "There's no point even bringing up Sabrina Page and Alden Shandy because their children died young. As did Sabrina."

"Then why did you bring them up, dear?" Nora inquired with ferocious sweetness.

"Nora, I'd never have believed you were such a snob. I'm not suggesting Ellery get into bed with that family—"

"He'll be the only Page who hasn't." Mr. Starling was sorting through the remaining cookies.

"That is *not* true," Nora stated, and the others loudly agreed. Many disapproving looks were directed at Mr. Starling.

Mr. Starling snickered and selected a crispy oatmeal Johnnycake.

Ellery thought uneasily back to the beginning of the conversation. "Who were the parents of Oliver, Barry, Violet, Lowell, Sidney, Everett, Virgil, and Daisy?"

Everyone seemed to be waiting for someone else to answer.

Kingston said, "In 1900, Samantha Page, who was Eudora's great-aunt, married Hamilton Shandy, and they had eight children."

Nora said, "Samantha wouldn't have been Eudora's great-aunt. She would be her great-cousin."

"No, I believe—"

"But that's the same thing as a first cousin once removed," Mrs. Ferris said.

"I don't see that it matters, dear."

Neither did Ellery. He phoned for the island taxi, gathered up Watson, and departed.

The Silver Sleuths were still arguing over his familial connections when the brass bell chimed behind him.

"Gangland slaying," Ezra Christmas was saying as Ellery and Watson climbed out of his taxi. "You see if I'm not right."

"Was Tackle Shandy in a gang?" Ellery was being polite. He was pretty sure Tackle had not belonged to any gang. Unless you counted his family.

"Probably. Those Shandys are a bad lot." Ezra beamed at the tip Ellery handed over. "The old girl is sure coming along." He nodded toward Captain's Seat, looking stately and ageless in the afternoon's golden light. "Just like the old days."

Ezra was elderly, but he couldn't be old enough to remember Captain's Seat *old* days.

"It's a work in progress."

"You can say that again." Ezra touched the brim of his chauffeur's cap and proceeded to sedately reverse down the entire length of the drive.

Ellery waved farewell as the chauffeur's cap grew smaller and smaller, and then he turned toward the steps. He couldn't help a quick look at the second-floor windows.

Sure enough, sunlight's reflection blazed in the panes of glass.

Granted, last night's sighting—no, sighting was too specific. Last night's optical illusion had happened a few hours later, but still. He was more than happy to accept Jack's explanation for that perplexing light.

Watson took off to inform the squirrels he was in residence again. Ellery unlocked the front door and went inside. Once again, he was greeted by the smell of paint and sawdust and glue. If possible, the house felt even quieter than it had the day before.

It seemed a lifetime ago that he had found Tackle sitting on his front steps.

He picked yesterday's ignored mail from the floor, went into the kitchen, and sorted through the bills and postcards. There was a brief note from Dylan, a chatty mini-travelogue from his mother (she and George were currently on location in British Columbia), and a *Wish you were here* from Robert Mane, who was visiting family in Oregon.

Robert's card went straight into the trash. Ellery liked Robert a lot, but that greeting was bound to irritate Jack. In a perfect world, Robert would meet someone terrific on vacation and Ellery could enjoy his friendship without having to worry about making Jack jealous.

Besides, Robert was lonely. Ellery knew too well how it felt.

He glanced out the window. Watson was comfortably curled in one of the new flower beds, blinking sleepily in the sunlight as he kept watch on the squirrel tree.

Ellery smiled reluctantly, shook his head, and considered his plans for the evening. At some point, he'd be hungry, but right now he still had the image of Tackle's body front and center in his brain.

Keeping too busy to think would be the best remedy for that.

There were still a couple of hours of daylight. If he was going down to the basement, now would be the time.

Was he going down to the basement?

He weighed it.

It would be very helpful to have Great-great-great-aunt Eudora's own perspective on her life for a change, without relying on the memories of people who'd known her as children. He'd been ruminating last night about where those journals might be stashed, and he thought he might have an idea of their general location.

On the other hand, he really hated crawling around damp, spider-ridden spaces. Not least because he had a tendency of getting locked inside them.

But this time of year, most of the spiders would be sleeping, right? Hopefully. And if someone was lurking inside his house, he probably had bigger worries than getting locked in the basement.

"Yeah, let's do it," he muttered, and went past the pantry to the door leading down to the wine cellar and the basement beyond.

The good news was, the basement light worked.

The bad news was, he could see how dusty and covered in cobwebs everything was.

But his vague memory of where the box containing his aunt's journals was stashed turned out to be correct. He found the box. He found the journals. And when he flipped open the pages of 1972, he was relieved to see that Eudora had been keeping an actual diary with a detailed record of her—dauntingly busy—daily life as well as her thoughts and feelings.

Yes, she still showed an alarming proclivity for clipping the occasional poem or cat cartoon, but overall, it seemed to be the diary of an ordinary woman living an ordinary life.

This is the longest year ever. (She was being literal. Leap year 1972 had been two seconds longer than any other year in recorded history.)

Congress has voted to send the Equal Rights Amendment to the states for ratification. (Don't set your heart on that one, Eudora.)

Went to see Fritz the Cat. *Not what I expected.* (Ellery inhaled so much dust, he saw his life flash before his eyes.)

In short, a treasure trove.

Would it hold the answer to Vernon Shandy's disappearance? That was probably too much to hope for. But if he could find the journal from 1963, it would certainly be a starting point for determining what, if any, role Eudora had played.

Ellery tossed 1972 back in with the other volumes, heaved the box into his arms, and staggered back up the stairs.

He reached the hall off the kitchen in time to hear his cell phone ringing. It took him a moment to locate it in the pile of bills on the table.

He did not recognize the number, but pressed Accept.

"This is Ellery."

There was a pause and then, "Is this Mr. Page?"

The stiff voice on the other end of the line was the same voice that had left Ellery that highly incensed message on the Crow's Nest answering machine. The kind of voice that would use the words *highly incensed* in ordinary conversation.

Ellery repeated cautiously, "Yes. Speaking."

"This is James Franklin."

"Mr. Franklin, I want to apologize again. I'm very sorry for—"

Franklin's voice shot up an aggrieved notch. "My mother is very old and very frail. She gets easily confused. She wouldn't be of any use in your investigation."

"It's not really an investigation—"

"Oh, *please*," Franklin interrupted. "Your reputation precedes you. And even if it didn't, Mrs. Crane is good friends with Sue Lewis. Sue Lewis of the *Scuttlebutt Weekly.*"

"I'm familiar with Sue."

"And *she* is familiar with you."

Ellery couldn't help a huff of amusement. He said, "Okay. I understand where you're coming from. I want to point out, though, that your mother invited me to visit her. I didn't break into her room. I didn't hold her hostage. If she was upset by my visit, I sure couldn't tell."

Franklin began to sound defensive. "Maybe not, but that isn't your call to make. My mother is not well. She can't take any sudden shocks."

Maybe that was true. Joey had seemed sturdy enough, all things considered, but Ellery would be the first to admit he was no medical expert. "I don't think I said anything to shock her, or even surprise her, but again, I'm very sorry if I upset her or you or Mrs. Crane. That wasn't my intention. I promise not to trouble your mother again."

Franklin made a fretful *hrmph*. "Why did you want to talk to her? That's what I don't understand. She doesn't know anything about that treasure."

That treasure?

Was that what everyone thought he was up to? If so, maybe that was a good thing.

"No, of course not," Ellery said. "But she worked at the Deep Dive, and from what I understand, that was home base for the Shandys."

"Oh yes," Franklin said bitterly. "You couldn't walk into the place without tripping over a Shandy."

How would he know? Hadn't he been a kid at the time?

"Well, they did own and run the pub, so I guess that makes sense."

There was a pause while Franklin fortified himself with a beverage. Ellery could hear the *clink* of ice against glass. Granted, Franklin could be enjoying a nice, bubbly sarsaparilla. Or did that only exist in movies?

When Franklin spoke again, he sounded less indignant. "I'm sure you know my mother was good friends with Vernon."

"She did say something to that effect."

"I imagine so. Well, I can assure you, he wasn't talking about diving for shipwrecks with her. Or with any woman, except, possibly, your aunt."

"I see."

Did Franklin realize he'd told Ellery more in a minute and a half than his mother had their entire visit?

"Don't draw the wrong conclusion. My mother was too smart to take Vernon seriously. She wasn't one of his conquests. To be honest, I think men like Vernon secretly hate women."

"I...couldn't speak to that."

Franklin paused for another sip, then said, "Did Vera Shandy really tell you to talk to my mother?"

"She really did, yes. She said your mother worked at the Deep Dive for a long time and knew everybody. Even if your mother doesn't remember much, she still might have insights into—"

Franklin cut in. "I can't have you getting my mother all worked up, but if you were serious about wanting to interview *me*, I'd be happy to meet with you. I do remember quite a bit from those days."

"Do you? How old were you?"

"When?"

Ellery rephrased his original thought. "When your mother worked at the original Deep Dive."

"I'd have been around eight. But it was different in those days. The pub, I mean, but also liquor laws. I could sit in the backroom and read or play or simply listen to the adults talk, and no one paid me any attention. I think half the time no one even knew I was there. Some of the other servers' kids did as well. Childcare wasn't a thing back then."

Really?

Franklin added, "To be honest, I probably remember much more about that time than my mother."

"That would be great," Ellery said automatically, although he had his doubts.

"I think it could be very useful." Maybe it was the sarsaparilla talking, but Franklin sounded more relaxed, almost cordial. "When would you like to get together?"

"Are you free for lunch tomorrow?"

"No. I'm sorry. I work as a travel agent in Newport. What about tomorrow evening?"

In theory, the Silver Sleuths were holding their emergency meeting tomorrow night, but after that afternoon's emergency meeting, Ellery thought perhaps he would pass and get the official minutes from Nora.

Nora and Kingston, because he now realized Nora, for whatever reason, was going to curate information for him.

Franklin was saying, "In fact, we could meet at the Deep Dive, if you like."

"Sure," Ellery said. "I've never been."

Franklin tittered. "No? Well, you're in for an experience. Shall we meet around nine? That's when things start to get interesting."

"Monday at nine."

"At the Deep Dive," Franklin said.

"At the Deep Dive," Ellery agreed.

CHAPTER FIFTEEN

Sunday Night

Today someone tried to kill me.

Ellery, lying in the miniature galleon of his bed, jumped at the sound of the maple tree outside his window, scratching against the glass. Watson, curled between his feet, slumbered peacefully on.

He glanced at the date written at the top of the page in Great-great-great-aunt Eudora's machine-precise script. In the later years of her life, her handwriting had grown as erratic as some of her behaviors, but in her thirties, Eudora's penmanship had been a thing of beauty.

This journal had been written in autumn 1964. Ellery had been unable to locate a journal for 1963. It seemed suspicious. The journals for '61, '62, '65, and '66 had all been found in order in the box he had dragged up from the basement.

Only 1963 appeared to be missing.

Because it contained incriminating evidence?

Or because Great-great-great-aunt Eudora had dropped it in the goldfish pond that had once graced the old rose garden?

She did appear to be a little accident prone. In 1962, she'd sprained her ankle in a fall down the grand staircase, and—reading ahead—it looked like she'd broken her wrist in 1964 when some unknown person ran her bicycle off the road.

What Ellery couldn't decide was whether this person really was unknown to Eudora or whether she, puzzlingly, chose not to name them. He suspected the latter.

But why? Why would Eudora keep that information to herself?

It was odd.

But after 1962, Eudora's journals *were* odd. Or at least, different in mood.

The witty, light-hearted tone was gone. She was still dutifully writing about the same things as she went about her same life, but something had definitely changed.

She had been happy.

And then she was not.

An obvious explanation was the disappearance of Vernon Shandy.

Ellery glanced up at the bewigged and steely-eyed life-sized portrait of his distant ancestor Captain Horatio Page, and then jumped as his cell phone rang.

Jack.

His heart lightened. He answered, "Hi. I was hoping you'd call."

"Are you at my place, by any chance?"

"No. Why?"

"I'm just checking in, making sure everything is okay."

Jack's tone sounded a bit off, and Ellery said, "It was thirty seconds ago. *Now* I'm nervous."

"Yeah. Well."

"Was that supposed to be reassurance? Because...not so much."

"I'm looking at the preliminary autopsy report on Tackle Shandy."

"Oh."

"As expected, Tackle was run over." Jack's tone was flat. "Then backed over."

It took two swallows before Ellery managed, "*Backed* over?"

"Yes."

"That's...an unpleasant thought."

"It's pretty gruesome. I'd like you to do me a favor and double check that every door and every window in that house is secure. Will you do that for me?"

"I'll do that for you and me both."

"There's no concrete reason to believe Tackle's death has anything to do with you finding those doubloons or whatever happened to Vernon sixty years ago. Tackle led a very messy life, and that can catch up with someone."

"Sure," Ellery said faintly.

"But it's not going to hurt to be extra careful until we get this thing wrapped up."

"You had me at *backed over.*"

"The bright spot is we have *a lot* of forensic evidence."

"You do?"

"Yes. It looks like a rage killing to me because whoever did this was not making any effort to conceal their tracks. And I mean that literally."

Ellery glanced at the journal lying face up on the bed. Fifty-eight years later? That had to be a coincidence.

But as coincidences went, it was an uncanny one.

"That's reassuring." Ellery was pretty sure his tone didn't convince either of them.

"After you finish checking all the doors and all the windows, text me back. I'll probably be in a meeting, but I'll be watching for your text."

"Right. Okay."

Jack said lightly, "I'm just being extra careful. You know me. I'm all about safety violations and security hardware."

Ellery smiled because that was true, but he also knew Jack well enough to know when he was genuinely concerned.

"I'll text you back in about ten minutes."

"Thank you. Have a good night. I'll talk to you tomorrow."

Ellery clicked off, threw back the covers, to Watson's confused delight, and headed into the drafty hallway.

"No, we're not playing," he told Watson, who snatched up his plushy lamb and followed. "This is not a game. This is not a drill."

The plushy lamb concurred, crying out in loud, harrowing *peeps* as Watson trotted after. Ellery rocked to a stop, and Watson crashed into his legs.

At the end of the long hall, lamplight shone from the sitting room, pooling on the faded carpet.

It was not moonlight or starlight. It sure as hell was not sunlight.

It was lamplight. Light from a lamp that was turned off and unplugged.

Ellery's heart, which was already thumping briskly, broke into a full gallop.

"This is *ridiculous.*"

He tried to tell himself he was angry, but honestly? He was—he hated to say *scared*—but he was pretty damned alarmed. If not actually freaked out.

But come *on*, already. Was the place now haunted? Because enough was enough.

Ellery strode down the hall toward the sitting room, and about one door down, the light in the room went out, leaving the hallway in almost pitch darkness.

He faltered, but made himself keep walking, one foot after the other. It wasn't easy. His knees were shaking in a way he couldn't remember since early childhood. His heart was pounding so hard, he felt like he was going to smother.

Watson had stopped at the head of the staircase and was whimpering.

Ellery reached the doorway and grabbed onto the frame for support. He was not imagining that creepy chill. The little room felt like a refrigerator. And he *did* smell roses.

He said firmly, although he could hear the embarrassing waver in his voice, "I don't know who you are. I don't know what you want. You're going to have to find a better way to communicate because you're scaring us. Unless that's the point."

As his eyes adjusted to the dark, he could pick out shapes within the moonlit room: the black rectangles of space on empty shelves, the glint of the brass finial of the lamp, the gleam of the rocker's headrest. His heart froze in his chest. He could just make out the silhouette of someone—something—sitting in the chair.

"Please don't do that."

The shadow did not move. That was just as well. If the rocking chair had creaked, if that shadow has so much as *quivered*, he'd have shot through the roof like a rocket.

"If you're...family, I *know* you didn't...wouldn't. I know and I'm trying to-to help."

Silence.

A silence as dark and bottomless as the floor of the ocean. As the yawning grave.

"I'm doing the best I can," he whispered.

Wait. He peered more closely. He was starting to imagine things. There was nothing in that room but moonlight and shadows.

From down the hall, Watson began to howl.

Ellery backed out of the doorway, turned, and sprinted down the hall. He said breathlessly, "It's okay, buddy. I'm seeing things." He felt around for the light switch, and tired light from a crystal light fixture illuminated the long, empty hall.

Fueled by adrenaline, he made his rounds in seven minutes, racing down the hall, then leaping into bed and checking his phone as his cell phone dinged with a text from Jack.

???

Ellery texted back: **Hatches battened. Bilges pumped.** Which probably did not mean what he thought it did, but whatever. If he texted: **I think the house is haunted**, Jack would think he'd lost it.

After a couple of seconds Jack texted: **xo.**

And just like that everything was okay again. Ellery could even laugh at himself.

A little.

Monday morning was so utterly ordinary, Ellery felt as though he'd stumbled into an alternate universe.

It was Kingston's day off, so Ellery and Nora spent the morning doing bookstore stuff. Or at least, trying to remember how to do bookstore stuff.

Nora filled in the gaps of their much-picked over Halloween-themed collection—and prepared for the soon to follow sale of that same collection. Ellery did payroll, placed a few small orders with publishers, and tried to hunt down a couple of out-of-print special requests.

All morning long, "customers" wandered in and out. Most were conscientious enough to buy *something*—more often than not small mystery-themed gift items rather than an actual book—but the real purpose of these visits was to gossip about Ellery's shocking find the previous afternoon.

From a bookseller's POV, it was exasperating. But from an amateur sleuth's POV, this slow trickle of opinion and information was actually pretty useful.

Public opinion leaned toward the theory that one of Tackle's criminal associates from the mainland had traveled to Pirate's Cove to "take him out." One or two people suggested a fatal family quarrel, although this was usually contested by other armchair detectives who insisted the Shandys never turned on each other.

"There's some truth to that," Nora told Ellery as the doorbell chimed farewell behind Elinor Christmas. "The Shandys may feud with each other, but in four hundred years there's been no record of any Shandy laying hand on another."

"Just because there's no record doesn't mean it didn't happen."

Nora's gaze was approving. "Very true, dearie. But in this case, what would be the motive?"

"Pirate's treasure."

"It's a good motive in itself, yes. But."

"He broke in both here and at Captain's Seat trying to retrieve those gold coins."

"There's no question Tackle would have done anything and everything he could think of to lay his hands on that treasure. But the Shandys would surely know better than anyone how you ended up with those coins. They'd also know Tackle had no clue where the treasure is hidden. *If* it's hidden anywhere. The assumption that the coins indicate a greater treasure could be totally false. The coins might be all there is."

Ellery thought that over and made a face. "True." He said ruefully, "It turns out I want to believe in the lost treasure of the *Blood Red Rose* as much as anyone."

"Of course you do. It's a wonderful legend."

"Okay, well, maybe Tackle's death has nothing to do with the treasure. Maybe his wife killed him for reasons we don't know. For...spending all his time hunting for treasure instead of mowing the lawn."

Nora's eyes twinkled. "You present a convincing argument."

"Wives and husbands are always the prime suspects."

"True. And June Shandy had to put up with a great deal from Tackle."

"Do they have children?"

"Thankfully, no."

Late morning, the wind from the west picked up strength, and Sue Lewis blew in.

The owner and editor of the *Scuttlebutt Weekly* was around Ellery's age, a pretty and petite blonde with brown eyes and olive complexion. She was always coiffed, always perfectly made up, and always on the hunt for a news story.

"Hello, Nora. Hello, Ellery." If Sue felt any discomfort strolling into enemy territory, she sure didn't show it. She walked right up to the sales desk, offered her best smile, and said to Ellery, "Can I buy you a cup of coffee?"

"I really caa—*oww*!" Ellery jumped as Nora, under cover of the tall sales desk, pinched his side. He glared at her.

Nora beamed at him, unmoved. "You go ahead, dearie. I've got this." She nodded to the otherwise empty store.

Sue kept her smile firmly in place. "Look, I'm trying to bury the hatchet."

"That's what I'm afraid of." Ellery shot Nora a warning glance, and she subsided.

"You could at least meet me halfway."

Ellery hesitated. The truth was, he didn't like confrontation, and the ongoing feud with Sue did bother him. At the same time, he had good reason not to trust her. "I don't want to be interviewed—"

She sighed. "I'm not going to interview you."

"—under the pretense of calling a truce."

"Ellery, I really *am* trying to call a truce." In a funny way, Sue's mounting irritation was more convincing than any show of syrupy sincerity would have been.

Watson sniffed Sue's immaculately pedicured toes peeping from her sandals, then delicately licked them. Sue squeaked and then laughed.

It was a giggly sort of laugh, and combined with the half-sheepish, half-defensive look she threw him, it disarmed Ellery.

"Oh, all *right*," he muttered.

"Gracious in defeat." Nora patted his back. "You two have a nice chat."

They ended up at a little stand on the pier.

Sue insisted on buying their coffee, and they settled at one of the many empty tables on the half-sheltered patio. It was a cloudy day, and the breeze was sharp. Sue huddled into her leather jacket, folded her arms, and regarded Ellery as though he presented a problem she simply couldn't figure out.

Ellery held up his cup. "Cheers." He took a mouthful of blessedly hot coffee.

Sue drew in a long breath and let it out very slowly as recommended by iBreathe. "I know we've had some…awkward moments in the past."

Ellery raised his brows. "Are you referring to the libel or the slander?"

"Just for a minute, look at things from the point of view of a journalist. From the minute you arrived on this island, people started dropping like flies."

Ellery gaped at her. "I arrived on the island in February. Nobody died until May."

Sue's smile was twisted. "It's adorable you think that's in your favor."

"Also, I want to point out, nearly every investigation I've been dragged into is connected to an older crime that went unnoticed."

"It looks more half-and-half to me. You can't pretend that you don't end up in the center of these investigations with suspicious frequency."

"I think it's because I'm an outsider. I see things from a different perspective."

"Jack's an outsider too, but he's not tripping over cold cases left and right."

"Jack's busy solving—and preventing—current crimes. Nobody's inviting the chief of police to stroll through their family secrets or…or whatever."

Sue made a noncommittal noise and sipped her coffee. "Jack said you're a catalyst."

"When did he say that?"

"Last June. After Brandon Abbott. He asked me to lay off you. That you weren't any more of a suspect than anyone else. Which was *patently* untrue."

Surprise held Ellery silent. Sue was referring to the painful interval when Jack had decided against pursuing a relationship with him. Not only that, but as far as Ellery could tell, Jack *had* considered him the prime suspect in Brandon's death. It was unexpectedly comforting to know that behind the scenes, Jack had tried to intercede on his behalf.

"I notice you didn't listen to him."

Sue's smile was sour. "No. It was the worst move he could have made."

Ellery said nothing. Sue's thinly—and not so thinly—veiled accusations in the *Scuttlebutt Weekly* had been extremely painful. She had done her best to ruin both him and his business. He had insight into why her attacks had become so personal, but it was still not easy to forgive.

As if reading his mind, Sue said, "You know, I spend all my time searching for interesting crime stories to cover. Meanwhile, you're stumbling into cold cases left and right. People *bring* their mysteries to you. The one time I actually uncover..." She gave a little gulp and stared out at the water.

Yeah, he did sympathize with her there. That would have been awful, and it was a good reminder of the trouble sleuthing could lead you into.

Ellery cleared his throat, which seemed to snap Sue out of her grim thoughts.

"Also, for the record, I think Jack could have been a bit more forthcoming about...what he was looking for. I don't think he deliberately misled anyone, but." She clamped her lips on the rest of it.

"I don't think he was *looking* for anything," Ellery said honestly.

"Oh please. Within the space of eight months, the two of you are practically living together."

Close but no cigar. Ellery kept that thought to himself.

Sue said briskly, "Anyway, that's neither here nor there. What I wanted to say was, I'm sorry if I was unduly…suspicious of you and that I published my suspicions as they occurred rather than waiting for corroboration."

"Okay," he said cautiously. "I accept your apology. Thank you."

"Moving forward, I think we could be of help to each other. I mean, it's kind of ridiculous that you've got poor little Mr. Peabody skulking around the newspaper archives instead of just telling me what you need."

Ellery opened his mouth, but she headed him off. "I have access to information you don't. I have resources you don't. And, much as I hate to admit it, vice versa. What I'm suggesting is if you help me, I'll help you."

Ellery's suspicions flooded back. "Help you how?"

"If, at the end of your investigation into Vernon Shandy's disappearance, you promise to give me your side of the story, whatever that story turns out to be, I'll wait to publish anything about what you're up to." Her gaze held his. "For example, I won't print Frances Crane's opinion of you sneaking in to see Joey Franklin at Sunset Shores. I won't, for example, speculate publicly as to why you might have wanted to talk to her."

"If you did, it would be pretty irresponsible."

Sue raised her shoulders in a that's-what-you-say. "And, as a show of good faith, I can confirm for you that Joey *was* having an affair with Vernon."

"That's not news."

"And that her husband knew about it."

"I figured that out already."

"And that Joey was *insanely* jealous of your aunt Eudora."

Ellery frowned. "Where did you hear that? James?"

Sue rolled her eyes. "*James?* No way. James believes Mommy Dearest was pure as the driven snow. No, I got it straight from my nana, who was a waitress at the Deep Dive the same time as Joey." She grinned at Ellery's expression. "By the way, Vernon also hit on my nana. Apparently, he was willing to boink anything in a skirt."

"I'm starting to get that picture." He added suspiciously, "Who's your nana?"

"Joan Lewis." Sue looked torn between disbelief and amusement. "Not everyone on this island is involved in a life of crime, you know. My nana was a wonderful mother and grandmother and homemaker. She was probably even a good waitress. Other than being a witness, she's not relevant to the case."

"Okay, okay."

"It was the Fourth of July, and the pub was officially closed. But the Shandys held a private party. Now here's something I'm sure you don't know. Joey believed she and Vernon were going to run away together that night."

"Why would she think that?"

"Vernon had a marriage license. She caught a glimpse of it in his wallet, I guess."

Ellery whistled soundlessly. "But wasn't she already married?"

"Yes, but they were separated."

"She was still technically married."

"In case you didn't notice, Joey lives in a world of her own."

Ellery *hadn't* noticed that. He knew Joey was prevaricating a bit, exaggerating a little, but she hadn't seemed delusional. He said, "Obviously, they didn't run off together."

"No. By the—to quote my nana—*shank's end of the evening*, Joey was drunk off her cute little ass. She and Vernon had a huge shouting match, and he left the party. Never to be seen again."

"How reliable a source is your nana?"

"She passed two years ago, I'm sad to say, but she was very reliable. For one thing, she didn't drink. At all. She was probably the only person at the Deep Dive that evening who was stone-cold sober."

"Did Joey follow Vernon out?"

Sue shook her head regretfully. "No. According to multiple witnesses, she was there until closing. Well, in theory she was working, but it sounds like the staff was partying as hard as the customers that night."

"Maybe Vernon came back to the pub."

"Maybe. It would have been after-hours. And why would he?"

"Did your nana know what Joey and Vernon argued about?"

"Joey's version was she refused to run away with Vernon. Among other things, she couldn't allow him to throw his Navy career away." Sue gave another of those ladylike snorts.

Ellery eyed her speculatively, "And what was your nana's theory?"

"According to Nana, Joey was *crazy* about Vernon. If he'd asked her to jump off a cliff with him, she'd have done it. So, had he asked her to run away with him, there's no way she'd have turned him down."

"What did Joey think happened to him?"

"She believed, *said* she believed, he killed himself in despair when she turned him down."

"From the little I know of Vernon, that seems highly unlikely."

"I'll say. No way did big, tough, treasure-hunting Vernon Shandy dive into the sea because hot-to-trot Joey Franklin wouldn't elope with him. He, at least, would know the marriage wouldn't be valid."

"Maybe he didn't care."

"He cared. He wouldn't have thrown his naval career away either."

Ellery said slowly, "You've been working on this case for a long time, haven't you?"

Sue's eyes kindled with a mix of emotions. "I sure have. I've been putting this puzzle together, piece by piece, for the last *three* years. And who gets a personal invite from the Shandys to stick his oar in? *You.* Vera Shandy won't even take my phone calls."

He smiled ruefully. "Sorry."

"Oh, it's not your fault," she said irritably. "I learned a long time ago life isn't fair."

Ellery weighed the pros and cons of working with Sue. He still didn't trust her, but that didn't mean she wasn't making a sincere effort to mend fences. She had volunteered a lot of useful information with no promise of anything in return.

He sighed. "I hope I don't regret this. But okay, I agree. It makes sense to work together this time."

Sue brightened. "Yes? I get an exclusive on the story?"

Ellery laughed. "I don't think you've got a lot of competition, but sure."

"*Excellent.*"

Her cat-that-got-the-cream smile made him uneasy, but he asked anyway. "Did your nana have any theory as to the other name on that marriage license?"

His unease grew as Sue's smile turned slightly malicious. "She sure did. She was convinced your great-great-great-aunt Eudora was the other name."

Ellery stared. "Vernon was planning to marry Eudora?"

"It went through his mind, obviously. That doesn't mean he was really going to do it. Or that *she* had any interest in marrying him. Vernon didn't seem to have been the settling down kind. Frankly, neither did she. But for years, the rumor was, he left the Deep Dive that night to go see your aunt Eudora."

CHAPTER SIXTEEN

The Shandys were in mourning.

That thought hadn't occurred to Ellery, though it probably should have, until he walked past Vera's house and found every available parking space filled.

There were a number of questions he wanted to ask the Shandy matriarch, starting with: *why did you hide the doubloons with that antique deep diving suit and then stash them in the Historical Society's warehouse*? But this was clearly not the time.

In any case, he thought he knew the answer. He just wanted confirmation.

In the meantime, he decided to head over to PICO PD on the slim chance that Jack could get away for lunch.

When he stepped through the glass doors, Mac, the grizzled desk sergeant, looked up and greeted him with a resigned, "Here comes trouble."

"Is he in a meeting?"

"I guess he is now." But Mac was smiling a little as he bent over his paperwork.

Ellery rapped on the half-open door to Jack's office.

"Come," Jack called curtly.

Ellery poked his head in. "We interrupt this program to annoy you and make things generally more irritating."

Jack gave a short laugh. "Hey there. What's up?"

"I wondered if you might be able to get away for lunch?"

"Sorry. No. I'm waiting for a call from Colonel Giordano of the State Police."

Ellery pulled a face. "Okay. I figured."

He started to withdraw, but Jack said, "Pull up a chair. I'll share my roast beef sandwich with you."

"You sure?"

"I wouldn't ask if I wasn't sure."

"True enough."

Jack gave him a quizzical look.

Ellery took the chair on the other side of the desk and accepted the half sandwich Jack handed across.

"Coffee?" Jack asked.

Ellery shook his head. "I'm already wired for sound."

Jack buzzed his intercom and requested a sparkling water from the vending machine.

Ellery bit into the sandwich. *Mm.* Roast beef, horseradish cream, fontina cheese, microgreens, and arugula packed onto a toasty Kaiser bun. So good. He was hungrier than he realized. He'd been running late and hadn't had time for breakfast. He chewed, swallowed, said, "I thought you'd be happy to know that Sue Lewis and I called a truce."

Jack's brows shot up. "I'm glad to hear it. Who drafted the peace treaty?"

"Sue."

"Good for Sue."

Ellery made a face, and Jack chuckled. "Come on. We both know you didn't enjoy being at war with Sue. Besides, she can be a useful ally."

"Keep your friends close and your enemies closer."

Someone knocked on Jack's door.

"Come."

A young woman in an explorer uniform entered with a bottle of water. She set the water on Jack's desk, Jack handed her a dollar bill, she shot Ellery a curious look, and departed.

Between bites of sandwich and stealing french fries, Ellery filled Jack in on everything Sue had told him regarding the rumors surrounding Eudora and Vernon.

Jack listened and considered. "By the time I knew her, she was quite elderly. I couldn't begin to form an opinion. Does it seem likely she'd have run away with him?"

"I wouldn't have thought so, but Vera did say Vernon and my aunt were sweet on each other. She also said they fell out over his military service."

"*That's* what they fell out over?"

"I know. It seems like he'd have given her plenty of other cause for concern." Ellery swallowed a mouthful of water. "I started going through her journals last night. I got through most of 1964, and there's not one single word about Vernon."

"Hm."

"Also, her journal from 1963 is missing."

"Missing as in…?"

"As in it's the only missing volume in two decades worth of journals."

"Well, that could be significant. Or not."

"*Also*, also, I'm pretty sure my house is haunted."

Jack laughed. "Well, I've got some news too. Concerning the doubloons you found in the *Roussillon*."

"Are they real?"

"Ohhh yeah. They're real. 100% authentic." Jack lifted a couple of files and pulled out a sheet of notepaper. "I'm not even sure what half of this means, but the silver coin is a very rare high-grade French Jeton circa 1700. I think Jetons are actually some kind of token. The doubloons are dated 1611 Seville Assayer B. They're graded MS-64, which seems to have something to do with coins that are mostly uncirculated, so close to mint condition. Basically, they're museum pieces. Or should be. Oh, and your estimated value was a little on the low side."

Ellery blinked. "On the *low* side?"

"Yep. Each one of the gold pieces would be expected to fetch about one hundred and fifty grand were they to go to auction."

"Gulp."

"You can say that again. It's a little hair-raising to think of them lying in that cupboard for months."

"Is there any way to know if they came from the *Blood Red Rose*?"

"The type of coins and the dates are right. It's impossible to know for sure without a cargo manifest or bills of lading or other documentation. Unfortunately, we're dealing with a pirate vessel, and pirates aren't renowned for their book-keeping. Even if Captain Blood kept accurate accounts, which is highly unlikely, those records would have been lost when the ship went down."

"Well, that's a pretty good indicator."

"It is. But the *Blood Red Rose* wasn't the only pirate vessel calling these waters home."

"She's only one known to have sunk."

"Even that's a legend."

"True."

Jack's cheek creased. "It's a fun legend, I'll give you that. And if a sunken pirate ship is found off this coast, it's most likely going to be the *Blood Red Rose*."

"Now you're humoring me." Ellery leaned across to take a french fry, laughing softly when Jack held him in place for a moment and kissed him.

Jack released him, said briskly, "The next interesting question is who actually owns those coins."

"Uncle Sam, right?"

Jack had a funny expression. "Not necessarily. The *Roussillon* went down in 1956, twelve miles off the coast. She was a commercial vessel, and the company that owned her is long out of business."

Ellery stopped chewing. "Wait. What are you saying?"

"I'm saying you probably have as much claim to those coins as anyone."

"*Me?*"

"You found them."

"Yeah, but…"

"The circumstances of how they got to be there don't necessarily change the fact that they were there for you to find. That said, you should expect everyone from Uncle Sam to the Wallaces—*and* the Shandys—to lay claim."

Ellery stared. "Honestly, this is more than I can think about right now."

"Okay." Jack put his hands up in a don't-kill-the-messenger.

"How's *your* case coming?"

"Which case?" Jack's tone was wry.

"Tackle Shandy's homicide."

"It's coming. Like I said, we've got a treasure trove—" At Ellery's look of pain, Jack amended, "A fair bit of evidence to work with."

"Like what?"

"Distinct tire tracks, paint flecks and smears, and several firsthand accounts of June Shandy arguing with, and threatening to kill, Tackle."

"You think Tackle's wife killed him?"

"It's been known to happen."

Despite the fact that Ellery had once suggested that scenario as a possibility, he was genuinely startled. "You don't think Tackle's death has anything to do with Vernon or the treasure?"

"We're still looking at all the possibilities. But this is the most plausible scenario. We know June was arguing with Tackle over money. They were in financial hot water and increasingly desperate. It seems Vera had stopped doling out cash when she discovered Tackle was trying to rope Ned into another of his illegal activities."

"What illegal activities?"

"Take your pick. In this case, extortion."

"I see..."

Jack tipped his head, viewing Ellery. "You don't like that theory?"

"Like you say, it seems the most plausible. The most likely." He made a face. "It's not like I have a strong preference."

"I'm thinking about getting Ned into the police academy."

"Are you serious?"

"I am. Yeah. I think he's smart and resourceful and actually a pretty good kid. He needs some guidance, and he needs a direction in life."

"But doesn't he have a criminal record?"

"He does. But he doesn't have a felony conviction, and the other charges against him have been reduced."

"You really *are* serious."

"I believe there's an opportunity here to steer this kid onto the right path. A path that will be good for him and good for the community—" Jack's phone rang. "Here's my call."

Ellery nodded and rose.

Jack said, "Are you staying over tonight?"

"Yes. But I might be late. I'm supposed to meet James Franklin for drinks at the Deep Dive around nine. I might drop Watson off at your place first."

Jack's brows drew together, but he nodded, and said crisply into the receiver, "Chief Carson speaking."

CHAPTER SEVENTEEN

Ellery was walking back to the Crow's Nest when he remembered the hiding space in the trap door beneath the carpet in his bedroom.

Eudora did not seem to throw anything away. But if her diary from 1963 had contained sensitive or damaging information, she might very well have hidden it in one of Captain's Seat many secret places. What better secret place than her bedroom?

Accordingly, when he reached the Crow's Nest, he went straight to the parking area behind the store.

Arf. Arf. Arf.

He could hear Watson barking from inside the store. Ellery sighed. Hopefully, that was because Watson knew he was nearby and not the way he behaved every time Ellery left the bookshop.

He jumped in the baby-blue VW and headed out to Captain's Seat.

When he arrived at the house, he was relieved to see the front drive full of vans and trucks, so renovation had resumed. Maybe too relieved. It was going to be flipping ridiculous if he became nervous about staying on his own. He did not *really* believe Captain's Seat was haunted. Not in the light of day, anyway. But there was no question he felt better hearing the barrage of hammers and nail guns and footsteps stomping back and forth.

The banker's box of Vera's photos still sat against the wall, where Jack had stowed it for safekeeping. With everything that had happened, Ellery had completely forgotten about it. He made a mental note to grab the box when he left.

He ran up the staircase, greeting the painters on the second level. On impulse he asked the head guy to paint the little sitting room at the end of the hall.

"Sure. What color?"

"I don't care. Something bright and cheerful."

The man scratched his chin. "Okay. Like what? You mostly picked cool-toned greens and blues and ivories."

"I don't care. Anything."

One of the other painters leaned over and whispered something. The head guy brightened. "We've got some yellow ochre left over from another job. Will that do?"

"Perfect." Ellery continued on his way to the master bedroom. He stepped inside, locked the door behind him—*it's just the normal noises in here!*—and rolled aside the faded carpet.

The trap door was about the size of a coffin (now there was a cheery thought). Ellery pulled it open and, after a moment's hesitation—he *really* did not like spiders—dropped down to the tiny hidey-hole beneath.

The hiding space was not tall enough to stand upright in once the door was closed. But he had no intention of closing that door. Hand on the ledge, he squatted down—this was actually a terrific storage space; why didn't he clean it out and utilize it?—and studied the narrow shelves at the far end. Dust blanketed everything.

Everything and nothing.

Ellery's eyes watered, he sneezed, mopped his face on his sleeve, and took a closer look.

Nope. Nothing.

Damn. Well, really, what had he expected?

Or maybe...

He squatted down, peering. He should have brought a flashlight...

Hey...

He let go of the ledge, crawled forward.

"Eudora, you old fox..."

Below the shelves was a short space, and pressed flat against the wall, so that its binding wouldn't show, was a brown leather book.

Ellery carefully withdrew the journal and straightened. He gripped the ledge, vaulted out of the space, and sat down on the bare floor. He opened the journal about halfway and glanced at the date at the top of the page. In the shaft of fitful sunshine streaming through the window, he could see the clearly printed words *June 1963*.

His heart jumped. He hadn't really believed he was going to find it. Didn't believe the journal still existed.

He scanned the first sentence.

I can't believe I'm going to be a Navy wife.

When I said so to Vernon last night, he laughed, showed me the license again, and said, "There's no getting out of it now."

I don't want to get out of it. That's the truth.

Ellery sucked in a sharp breath, murmured, "Oh no."

Oh no, because whatever had happened, it wasn't good. Eudora had not ended up a Navy wife, and Vernon had disappeared off the face of the planet.

"Please don't be a murderess."

A little waft of paint-scented breeze—and roses?—from beneath the closed door stirred the pages.

Ellery glanced at his watch. He had left Nora alone at the bookshop for far too long. She'd be starving by now. He snapped shut the book, jumped to his feet, and went to the door.

Down the hall, the painters had already dragged the furniture out of the little sitting room. The bookshelves, rocker, and small table crowded the corridor. The small lamp lay on its side, its flowered globe in bits.

"What happened?"

The head guy looked apologetic. "Sorry. It got knocked over when we moved the rocker. It can probably be repaired."

Uh no, probably not. But there was no time to deal with it now.

Ellery hurried down the stairs, journal tucked under his arm. He grabbed the banker's box in the grand entry and hurried outside.

A few minutes later, the baby-blue VW was zipping down the road back to Pirate's Cove.

"Perhaps we should shelve Vernon's case for now and turn our attention to Tackle Shandy," Mrs. Nelson was saying when Ellery opened the door to the Crow's Nest.

Watson let out a cry of the heartbreak and betrayal of being left behind by someone who deliberately went on adventures without you, and raced to greet him. Ellery hastily set aside the box and journal on the rare-book display case.

"I know. I know. I'm sorry—" He managed not to sprawl flat on the floor beneath the onslaught.

Ignoring the mauling taking place before them, Nora replied, "Do you think so, dear? When we're so close to solving the case?"

"*Are* you?" Ellery kissed Watson's nose, put him aside, and rose with whatever dignity was available to a man wrestling on the floor with a puppy.

"But are we, dear?" Mrs. Clarence echoed.

Ellery glanced at Mrs. Clarence and did a double take. Mr. Starling stood beside her, drinking coffee. Were they *living* at the Crow's Nest now?

"Besides," Nora selected a taco from the box on the counter. "There's really no mystery about who killed Tackle Shandy."

"There isn't?"

"No, dearie. It's getting Chief Carson enough evidence to prove it in a court of law. *That's* the challenge."

Mrs. Nelson said, "For that matter, there's no mystery as to who killed Vernon."

"What am I missing? Who killed Vernon?" Ellery looked from Nora to Mrs. Nelson to Mrs. Clarence to Mr. Starling.

Mr. Starling took another mouthful of coffee.

"Joey Franklin, of course," Nora informed him kindly. "That's why James was so terrified when he left you that message. He knew you were closing in on his mother."

"I— He didn't sound terrified. He sounded irate and self-righteous."

"A man feels he's in the right when he's defending his mother," Mrs. Clarence assured him.

"But—"

Nora smiled. "Were you worried that Eudora was the culprit? Eudora was far too shrewd and sensible to ever fall for a man like Vernon Shandy. Besides, she'd known him her entire life. She knew him inside and out."

"Backward and forward," volunteered Mr. Starling.

"There's no romance in that," Nora assured Ellery. "No, dearie, Eudora would never have her head turned by a man like Vernon Shandy."

"What if Vernon was serious about Eudora?"

The Silver Sleuths exchanged doubtful and then uneasy glances.

"What if he really did love her?"

"That seems very unlikely," Mrs. Clarence said.

Mrs. Nelson looked at Mr. Starling. Mr. Starling looked at Nora. Nora chewed her lip.

Ellery asked, "Okay. So, who killed Tackle Shandy?"

Back on solid ground, the Silver Sleuths relaxed and began to talk at once.

"June," Mrs. Clarence said. "There's no question."

"The question is why they haven't arrested her yet," Mrs. Nelson said.

Mr. Starling retorted, "*Arrest* her? They ought to give the poor benighted creature a medal. What that woman had to put up with."

Nora, observing Ellery, asked, "What does Chief Carson say?"

"He says they're still looking at all the possibilities."

It gave them less than a moment's pause.

"He probably wouldn't tell you anyway," Mrs. Clarence said. "Sanctity of the confessional and all that."

"Chief Carson is not a priest, dear."

"He's definitely not a priest." Ellery examined the box of tacos on the sales desk. "Where did these come from?"

"Hermione and Edna were kind enough to bring me lunch."

"Sorry." Ellery meant it. "I totally lost track of time. But I meant, where did you find tacos on this island?"

"Oh! There's that new little *hacienda* where Gimcracks Antiques used to be."

"Authentic New England Mexican food." Ellery grinned.

"It's very delicious. Help yourself."

"That's okay. So listen, gang, we're not interfering or getting involved in any more ongoing police investigations. I gave Jack my word."

"I didn't give Jack *my* word," Mrs. Nelson replied.

"Nor I," Mrs. Clarence put in.

Nora admonished, "Now, dear, if Ellery gave his word, we must abide by that. Chief Carson could make life very unpleasant for all of us if he so chose."

Stanley Starling rubbed his jaw, as though recalling an instance of police brutality that had, in fact, never happened. "That's fine with me. I'm not forgetting what went down at the Black House even if you zanies are. I say we stick to cold cases from here on out."

Far from being chastened, the others began to recount their adventures.

"Absolutely. We'll wait for the police to finish their investigation, and *then* we'll solve the case," Nora concluded.

"I've created a monster." Ellery picked up the box and journal and retreated to his office.

As he sat down at his desk, his cell phone rang. He smiled at Jack's contact photo and pressed the green button. "What's up?"

"Did I hear you say you were having drinks with someone named James tonight?"

"It's just work, honey."

Jack spluttered, "Uh, right. And James is?"

"Joey Franklin's highly incensed son. Remember?"

"You got him from *highly incensed* to drinks-at-nine in less than twenty-four hours. You're good. I hope you won't mind if I run a background check on him."

It was not a question, and Ellery chuckled.

"In other news, I found Eudora's lost journal."

"You're on a roll."

"I didn't have a chance to do more than glance at it, but it seems like she and Vernon definitely talked about getting married. She thought it was for real. Who knows what was really going on with him?"

"Well, I think maybe he thought it was for real too. This jibes with what I was able to learn from the Navy. One reason they weren't immediately concerned when Vernon didn't turn up was because he'd applied for a couple of extra days' leave to get married."

"You contacted the Navy?"

He could hear the shrug in Jack's voice. "Eudora is family. If the truth about what happened between her and Vernon is important to you, it's important to me."

Why that brought a lump to Ellery's throat, he had no idea. But he said, a little huskily, "Thank you, Jack."

"Of course." The next minute Jack was back to business. "Remember to keep your phone with you at all times. I'll see you tonight."

CHAPTER EIGHTEEN

I gave the doubloons to Vera today.

I think the little fool thought it was an admission of guilt.

It doesn't matter. I know Vernon would want his family looked after, and this is the best I can do, given that they apparently believe me capable of murder. I suppose it's my own fault for wanting our marriage kept secret.

It was seven o'clock. The wind had picked up around four thirty, and it rustled around the rafters and knocked on the attic door of his office. Ellery had been reading Eudora's journal for most of the afternoon, and at that point he had a pretty good idea of what had happened to Vernon.

Or at least, Eudora had had a pretty good idea.

He'd had some bad moments, though. Moments when he'd been convinced Eudora had indeed killed her betrothed.

Starting with the fact that there were no journal entries from July fourth through the twenty-fifth. Eudora was a woman who had not missed a day of writing in her diary for over a decade, so that complete and absolute silence was hair-raising.

When she did resume her diary, it was as if Vernon had never existed.

There was no mention of him. None. Zero.

And then, in September, a haunting entry.

How could he do it? How? After everything. My dearest friend. My only love. I'll never understand. I lie awake night after night, trying to make sense of it. I can't eat. I can't sleep. I can't think of anything but why, why, why?

Father used to say, "A man is lucky if he is the first love of a woman. A woman is lucky if she is the last love of a man."

I thought he was so wrong. Now I know he was so right.

That was when Ellery became certain Eudora had killed Vernon. And while he was never going to be okay with that, her anguish was so intense and consuming, he couldn't help grieving with her.

But then came the entry of November 11. The entry that changed everything.

Vernon is dead.

I know that now.

How could I not know it before? What a fool. It's as though a fever broke and I can see clearly, think coolly again. Of course he's dead. Vernon would never leave me any more than I could leave him. If this terrible war couldn't separate us for long, nothing else could. Certainly, no other woman. I'm ashamed for ever thinking such a thing.

Was it easier to believe he'd run away than to accept he was dead?

He was never cruel. Never a coward. If he'd changed his mind, he'd have told me. We never lied to each other. Never.

Besides, he'd never have deserted. Why would he? He loved the Navy.

Joey killed him. I know it. I saw it in her eyes today when we ran into each other at the Royale. She was having lunch with her stepson, that poor child with the stammer and the charming habit of stealing change from everyone's jackets in the cloakroom at the Deep Dive. The excuse was the boy's birthday, but she was only there to show off her new hat. An idiotic thing that looked like a giant green thimble.

Joey hates me for what she did. She blames me. And I hate her. And blame her. I know what she did—and she knows that I know.

My only comfort is she's miserably unhappy.

Almost as unhappy as me.

Ellery let out a long careful breath. Instead of being relieved to learn Eudora was not guilty of murder, he felt like there was a weight on his heart.

"I don't think she ever got over it. I think it ruined the rest of her life."

Watson thumped his tail.

"As for Joey… It's not proof," Ellery said. "Eudora didn't see it happen. She doesn't know *what* happened. A couple of months earlier, she believed he'd run off with someone else. Just like everyone else thought. For all Eudora knew, Joey thought *she'd* killed Vernon."

Another patient tail thump from Watson.

A few days before Christmas, Eudora had handed the doubloons over to Vera, and that was the final mention of Vernon.

Sorting through the photos in Vera's box, which seemed to have all been taken that fateful summer, almost made it worse in that, until Ellery was staring at sunburned, smiling faces of people his own age, the characters in this drama had been just that: characters.

Now they were real people.

Now he knew his aunt Eudora had been beautiful. That she had dimples and curly black hair and a mischievous smile. That she favored cat-shaped sunglasses and bathing caps with blue flowers. He knew Vernon had gray-blue eyes and a grin that would be hard to resist—and that most of the time he was grinning at Eudora. Also, he couldn't help noticing, Vernon would not be an easy guy to take down, which made Ellery suspect that whatever had happened to him had happened when he wasn't paying attention—or from someone he didn't see as a threat (which was probably everyone).

He knew now that Vera had been really lovely, that her love for leopard print was nothing new, and that even back then, she had never been without a cigarette in her hand. He knew that her favorite seating arrangement was on Tony Bernard's lap, and that Tony Bernard looked at her like he still couldn't believe he'd got that lucky.

He now knew Tackle Shandy had looked just like his dad, Rocky, and that Barry Shandy did not like having his photo taken and was not shy about showing it.

And Ellery knew now that Joey Franklin had been what, in her day, they called *a dish*. She was a cuddly armful of beehive blonde hair and false eyelashes and pert full breasts barely contained by her (inevitable) pink polka-dot bikini top. He knew that Douglas Franklin was rarely without a cigarette, a drink, and a racing form (even when he was tending bar), and that he usually appeared to be hungover, which probably wasn't helped by the fact that his wife was usually posing for Vernon. In every single photo, Mr. and Mrs. Franklin both wore wedding rings. If they *were* separated, Ellery couldn't help thinking that no one had told Douglas.

Real people who had experienced real tragedy.

Oh, and then there was the Franklin boy, James. A skinny kid with a snub nose, Ed Grimley hair, and a permanently worried look on his pinched face. He was always hovering, like a little ghost, on the edge of those fading snapshots. In fact, half the time, he was partially cut out of the photo, so that there was nothing left but his small hand groping for something that wasn't there.

Ellery was on his way out the door to drop Watson off at Jack's and maybe take a quick shower and brush his teeth before meeting James at the Deep Dive, when Nora arrived.

"*Oh!* You gave me a start, dearie. You're working very late."

Ellery gazed beyond Nora to where Mrs. Nelson, Mrs. Clarence, Mrs. Ferris, Mr. Starling, and Kingston were lurking.

"I thought you already held your emergency Silver Sleuths meeting this afternoon." Ellery couldn't help adding, "And yesterday. And the day before."

"Er, we're in the midst of a case, dearie. Also, Mrs. Ferris wasn't able to join us earlier. And we must hear Kingston's report after his trip to the newspaper morgue."

Kingston smiled uncomfortably. "I don't want to raise anyone's expectations. I really didn't discover much."

"It's all part of the larger picture," Nora assured him.

"What did you find out?" Ellery asked.

Kingston opened his mouth, but Nora said quickly, "No, no. Not here. Let's go inside. We don't know who might be listening."

Given the frightening speed and reach of Pirate Cove's underground communication system, she had a point.

"I can't stay," Ellery said. "I'm on my way to meet James Franklin at the Deep Dive."

Kingston said, "*Ah.* Well, in that case. My information does concern the Franklins. Douglas had a criminal record for assault and battery. However, that was after he left the military and before his marriage to Josephine. He didn't have any further run-ins with the law after they married."

"Perhaps that's because no one called the cops on him," Nora said.

"Does Jack Carson know you're going to the Deep Dive?" Mrs. Nelson interrupted. Her expression was disapproving.

"Yes. Why?"

"*You're* going to the Deep Dive?" Nora gave her cohorts a pointed isn't-this-wonderful? look. "What a coincidence. *We're* going to the Deep Dive too!"

"We are?" Mr. Starling sounded uneasy. "When did we decide that?"

Nora said blithely, "Earlier."

"I've always wanted to go to the Deep Dive." Mrs. Ferris clapped her hands together.

"Me too!" Mrs. Clarence said.

Ellery broke in, "Nix. Nyet. No. *No*, you're not going to the Deep Dive. That is no place for you guys."

"It's no place for you either," Mr. Starling put in. He added, "Er, at least, from what I've heard."

"After all, you can't *stop* us, Ellery," Mrs. Clarence said. "We're not children."

"No. I can't stop you. But I'm asking you not to—or rather, I'm asking you to please *postpone* your visit so that I can, um, conduct my own operation without interference."

Nora seemed a little hurt. "We're not going to *interfere*, dearie. We're going to provide backup."

"I know, Nora, and I appreciate that, but—"

"Ellery's right. The Deep Dive is not the place for us," Mrs. Nelson broke in. "The drinks are *outrageously* overpriced, and the food is *very* greasy. According to my husband."

"We're not going there for dinner, dear."

"We can't sit in there and not eat or drink. They need the tables. They'll throw us out."

"Pshaw. At this time of year? They need the business."

"But we wouldn't be *giving* them business, Nora."

"We'll each order one drink and nurse it."

Mr. Starling said grimly, "I'm going to need a hell of a lot more than one drink to get me through this!"

"Can I just interrupt for a second?" Ellery pleaded. "It's going to be very distracting if you all show up there. If you really want to help—"

"Very well. Kingston and I will go," Nora announced.

Kingston cleared his throat. "My dear, I really don't think the Deep Dive is a suitable—"

"*No, you don't*, Nora Sweeny," Mrs. Nelson exclaimed. "You don't get to take over *our* case."

"I give up," Ellery said. "Come on, Watson."

He continued out the door and down the walk, leaving the Silver Sleuths to battle it out. He sincerely hoped he wouldn't be seeing all—or any—of them that evening, but that would probably require divine intervention.

Footsteps hurried down the walk after him. Kingston called, "Ellery?"

Ellery turned.

Kingston, slightly out of breath, caught him up. "I did have one more piece of information to share. It may or may not be relevant, but I think you should know that in 1985 Douglas Franklin was killed in a hit-and-run accident. They never caught the driver."

CHAPTER NINETEEN

The Deep Dive was all that Ellery had expected: dark, dingy, and perhaps a little dangerous.

James Franklin was not.

Not dark, not dingy, and not remotely dangerous. Also, not what Ellery expected.

Although, James must have been *a little* what Ellery expected, given that Ellery recognized him immediately. But then, like Ellery, James stood out like a sore thumb in the cave-like interior of the pub.

Until he walked into the Deep Dive, it hadn't really occurred to Ellery that there was any class division in Pirate's Cove. But the minute he pushed through the heavy double doors, he saw that the smoky interior (although surely in this day and age no one was actually smoking indoors?) was crowded with fishermen and farmers.

Not vacationing fishermen. The fishermen who provided the restaurants and markets with their fresh fish. And not the owners of flower nurseries or landlords of cozy B&Bs named North Light Farm or the Rose & Ivy. The farmers who got up at dawn to provide the dairy and meat and produce that supplied the restaurants and markets.

No one said or did anything at all threatening. Ellery got a few side-eyes, caught a few whispers. But really, it just added to the ambiance.

He located James seated at a table against a wall that was mostly taken up by a mounted swordfish the size of a dinghy. He—James, not the swordfish—raised a hand in greeting, and Ellery made his way through the tables and chairs, most of them filled, despite what Nora thought.

"James? I'm Ellery." Ellery offered his hand, James half rose, they shook, and Ellery took the seat on the other side of the table.

He'd been expecting someone who matched that aggrieved voice on the other end of the phone, but James Franklin was just an ordinary, pleasant-looking guy in his sixties. His fair hair was turning gray, and he was more chunky than stocky, but he had a nice smile. In the gloom, his eyes were a light, indeterminate color.

"You look a lot like your aunt Eudora," James said, and that answered that. He knew all about Ellery, so there was no point in continuing the pretense that he was writing a book. Frankly, that was for the best. Ellery hated lying.

"Do I? I've only recently seen pictures of her as a young woman."

"Oh yes," James said. "You look like her. Like all the Pages, which I guess, means you look like all the Shandys."

"Ha," said Ellery.

The bartender, who turned out to be Reg from the Salty Dog, came over to them and asked Ellery what he wanted to drink. James ordered another Wild Turkey on the rocks. Ellery ordered a beer, to keep life simple, but Reg said, "I can make that Blue Iceberg cocktail you like so much."

"Sure!" He did not plan on drinking a lot. He thought it would be wise to stay sharp.

When Reg stepped away, James said, "Did Vera really sic you on my mother?"

Why did he keep asking that? Why was it so hard to believe?

"I wouldn't phrase it like that."

"I would." James gave a narrow smile. "What does Vera think happened?"

"When?" Ellery asked blankly.

James said impatiently, "When Vernon died. What does Vera think happened?"

Ellery's scalp prickled. Okay, so right there. Right from go. *When Vernon died.* No question in James's mind about what happened to Vernon.

"She doesn't know. That's why she asked me to look into it. It was a long time ago, and everyone's memory is a little foggy."

"Not mine."

"Really? But you were pretty young."

"I was a good listener. Still am."

Reg returned with their drinks. Ellery paid, and Reg said, "You know, you're a long way from port, bucko."

Ellery winked. As Reg moved away, James asked, "What did that mean?"

"That I've never been here before. My friends and I gravitate toward the Salty Dog."

Surprisingly, James said, "I like this place. No one bothers you."

"That's right. You must know this place well. Your parents worked here after the original Deep Dive burned down."

"My mother worked here. My father got a job as a cook at the Blue Galleon. He was on the wagon by then."

"Good for him."

James smiled a chilly little smile. "You don't have to make small talk. We're here because we both want information."

Ellery began to wonder if coming to the Deep Dive alone had been such a great idea. Reg was right. He *was* a long way from port. Not that anything could happen to him in a public space.

"Okay. What do you remember about that night?" he asked.

"No. First you. What does Vera think happened?"

Ellery re-revised his opinion of James. He looked pleasant enough, but there was an edge to him. He might not be a bad man, but he was not a *nice* man. "Vera thinks someone killed Vernon the night he was supposed to elope with my aunt."

Glass midway to his lips, James froze. He stared over the rim at Ellery, and it was one of the weirdest, blackest looks Ellery had ever seen in a fellow human's eyes.

James put his glass down. "That's not correct. He wasn't going to marry your aunt. He wasn't going to marry anyone. He was having way too much fun to ever be satisfied with one woman. Men like that hate women."

Ellery shrugged. "Well, you were there. I wasn't."

James smiled another of those tight little smiles. "That's right." He picked up his glass and took a long swallow.

"Then again, you were a child, and you might not have always understood what was going on."

"I understood. I understood a lot more than anyone knew."

"Right. I'm just going by the fact that Eudora had filled out her part of the marriage license. She mentions it in her journal. And the fact that Vernon gave *her* those gold doubloons. She gave them back to Vera the December after he disappeared. When she knew for sure he was never coming back."

James's lips parted, but no sound came out. For one split second, he looked stricken. But a moment later, that expression changed to blazing fury.

"You're *lying*," he shouted.

But no one heard because at that instant, the door to the Deep Dive flew open and a troupe of itinerant vaudevillians entered. They seemed to be arguing with each other—loudly— possibly over the accident to their spaceship that had stranded them on Planet Earth. Never had Ellery seen so many handlebar mustaches and funny hats in one place before.

Nor had anyone else at the Deep Dive, and the newcomers had the attention of all.

"The Martians are coming!"

"Where'd your tour bus break down?" a man at the bar called.

This was greeted by laughter up and down the rail.

"When does the Big Top open?"

"Halloween's next week!"

"Do you know 'Ye Cannae Shove Yer Granny Off a Bus?'" called someone else.

"Too late!" his neighbor shouted back. "Looks like someone already did!"

More laughter.

Ellery sank lower in his chair. He glanced at James, and to his dismay, saw that he was on his feet and moving through the tables toward the hall entrance beneath a green EXIT sign.

He swore. Now what? They'd barely got started. James hadn't told him anything he didn't already suspect. He had no more proof than he'd had before he walked in the door. Should he go after him?

Oh hell. The mustachioed ringleader of the...of the... anyway, a person in a ridiculously oversized plaid coat, fedora and...clogs? was on the approach.

Clop-clop. Clop-clop.

"It's all right, he's only gone to the men's restroom," Nora hissed, reaching Ellery's table.

"Nora, are you out of your mind?" Ellery hissed back. "What are you doing? What are you *wearing*?"

"We had to turn to the Scallywag's costume department for our disguises."

"Why would you have to come in disguise? And such terrible disguises! You're *drawing* attention to yourselves."

Nora waved that idea off. "We had to take the risk. Kingston has some urgent information for you!"

Kingston, who'd made only the most feeble attempt to disguise his appearance, hovered behind Nora. He was shaking his head. "Nora, I've already told you that Ellery *knows*."

"But he doesn't know *everything*."

"But he does. I told him everything. Which was little enough."

Ellery heard the *squeak* of door hinges, saw a shadow slide along the section of the hall, coming toward the bar area. "Go. Away." He told Nora. "Now! Go!"

"Be careful!" Nora hissed as Kingston drew her away. "Remember Carroll Cole!"

"*Who?* Never mind!" He waved her off barely in time.

Clop-clop. Clop-clop.

Loud whispers floated from their table.

What did he say?

Does he want us to join him?

Is he all right?

Is he running a tab?

What should we order?

Ellery closed his eyes, shook his head. A few seconds later, James returned and took his seat across from Ellery. His face was pink and damp, his eyelashes sticky. He'd either been crying or splashing his face with water. Ellery guessed water.

"Are you okay?"

"Fine. It's very warm in here." James said apologetically, "I'm sorry I interrupted you. You were explaining why Vera thought my mother—who worked herself to the bone for that woman, by the way—could possibly have anything to do with killing Vernon."

"For one thing, a number of people heard them arguing that night. It seems like your mother might have seen that marriage certificate and maybe got the wrong idea?"

"That's it?" James rolled his eyes. "That's ridiculous. My mother was a happily married woman. She saw through Vernon from the first. There must be some other reason Vera targeted her."

"*Targeted* is too strong a word," Ellery said. "She was just one of the names on Vera's list."

"May I see the list?"

Ellery smiled. "I don't carry it around with me."

"No, of course not." James' smile matched Ellery's for insincerity. "When you went to see my mother, what did she tell you?"

"Probably more than she intended to."

James drew a breath and sat back in his chair. "No. You're lying again. I don't know what you think that's going to get you. My mother is old, and she gets mixed up. But even so, she couldn't tell you about something she never knew anything about."

Reg appeared at their table. "Another round?"

"Not for me," James said.

"I'll have another." As Ellery glanced past Reg, he spotted a familiar set of wide shoulders in a familiar leather jacket at the very end of the bar. His heart lifted.

As Reg moved away, James smiled at Ellery. "You really do love playing detective."

"Mostly I just get dragged into things."

"Oh, I doubt that."

"No, really. It's true. If I hadn't discovered my aunt's involvement with Vernon, I probably wouldn't have pursued this at all. I can't say I'm completely sorry, because it turns out my aunt was an interesting woman. And a kind woman. She didn't deserve what happened to her. She not only had to suffer through losing the man she loved, but also, a lot of people suspected she played a part in his death. I'd like to set the record straight if I can. I think maybe she would expect that."

James licked his lips. "I liked Eudora. She was nice to me. But bad things happen to good people. It's nobody's fault."

"Except we're not talking about cancer. We're talking about murder. That's *somebody's* fault."

Out of the corner of his eye, Ellery saw Jack rise from the bar and walk down the little hall. Over the babble of the Silver Sleuths seemingly ordering every appetizer on the menu, he heard the restroom door squeak open.

James asked casually, "Do you remember all the names on Vera's list?"

"There weren't that many, and I think we can now safely rule out Rocky and Barry."

James looked perfectly blank.

"Originally, there were six names: Eudora Page, Tony Bernard, Barry Shandy, Douglas Franklin, Joey Franklin, and..." Some impulse drove Ellery to add, "James Franklin."

James stared and then laughed. "I don't believe that for a minute. Vera never suspected me. No one suspected. Why would they?"

"Because you were always there listening in to everyone's conversations—and getting a lot of things wrong. Because you loved your step-mom very much and you were terrified that she was going to take off with Vernon and leave you with an alcoholic, compulsive-gambler father. Even if she'd wanted to take you with her, she couldn't. She couldn't legally take you from Douglas."

"He'd have never let her go. Never let either of us go."

"But you didn't know that. And you didn't know that Vernon had no intention of leaving with her anyway. Instead, you saw an opportunity and you grabbed it."

"What opportunity?" he asked thickly.

Ellery shook his head. "I don't know. I know that Vernon wouldn't consider you a threat. That he wouldn't be on guard with you. I think after the shouting match with your mother that night, Vernon went outside, and you followed him. And I would guess that maybe he sat down to have a smoke and cool off, and you came up behind him and hit him with something. And then, I think you went and told your father what you'd done, and he figured out some way to dispose of Vernon's body. You couldn't do that by yourself. The only people who'd be interested in protecting you would be your parents. There's no way your mother could have dragged a man the size of Vernon—and there's no way you'd have told her anyway. So that leaves you and your dad."

Jack had not yet returned to the bar, and Ellery felt a flicker of uneasiness. Surely Jack hadn't seen Ellery and James talking and drawn the conclusion that everything was fine?

Everything was not fine.

James was trying to make his mind up to take some course of action, and Ellery was unsure if he should play along and rely on Jack or if the Silver Sleuths were liable to try to rescue him and put themselves and everyone else in greater danger.

"It's very warm in here," James said. "I think we should step outside and get some fresh air."

Where are you, Jack?

"I think we should stay inside. Reg is bringing my drink now."

James said with a hint of his old irritability, "I think you should know that I'm pointing a thirty-eight special at you from under this table."

Ellery's heart seemed to deep dive into the pit of his stomach.

Was he? Both of his hands were under the table.

Ellery said with a calm he didn't feel, "If you shoot me in the middle of a room full of people, you're going to jail forever."

"I'm going to jail forever anyway if you go blabbing your mouth. This way, I can claim that the gun I carry for self-defense went off accidentally. Maybe I'll get away with it. It's definitely worth of a try."

It was tempting to say, *Go right ahead!* But what if James went right ahead?

Maybe James was bluffing. But maybe he wasn't. He had killed at least one person and maybe as many as three, including (Ellery was pretty sure) his own father.

Ellery's gaze flicked once more to Jack's empty barstool. *Seriously?*

Of all the times and all the places.

"Stand up, walk past my chair, and go down that hall to the exit. I'll be right behind you."

Ellery rose. He glanced at the table in the center of the room where the Silver Sleuths were— He did a double take.

The Silver Sleuths were so busy toasting each other and sharing bites of potato skins and onion rings, they hadn't even noticed he and James were leaving the pub!

He stepped past James, who also rose, and sticking close enough to Ellery to breathe down his neck, jammed something hard in the small of his back. Ellery flinched.

Maybe that gun wasn't real. But it sure *felt* real.

"Keep walking," James said. "You're doing great."

Ellery walked as slowly as possible down the short hall, James panting down his collar every step of the way. They reached the emergency exit, and Ellery shuffled to a stop.

"Go on. Don't stop now."

Ellery inhaled carefully, rested his hands on the crash bar, and pushed.

The door swung open, and sweet-salty night air rushed in. Ellery stepped outside.

A large fist fastened on the back of his jacket, and he was half swung, half hurled aside. He landed against the rough stone wall of the pub, unhurt but confused.

He had been unable to see what was happening behind him, but James's gasp was followed by an *oof* and the alarming *clang* of metal hitting concrete. James landed against the wall next to Ellery.

Jack, stony-faced and slit-eyed in the jaundiced glow of the security lights, yanked James's arms behind his back.

"James Franklin, you're under arrest for the murder of Tucker Shandy."

James opened his eyes, met Ellery's wide gaze, and started to laugh.

CHAPTER TWENTY

"**T**ackle Shandy? That's *it*? That's a little disappointing," Ellery said.

Jack gave him a pained look.

"I only mean, Tackle Shandy was simply the most recent victim."

"I know, and we'll continue building the case against him for Vernon's murder, but fifty-nine years later and without a body, it's a little more complicated. However, if we can get him for Tackle, we have a much better shot at getting him for Vernon."

"Because his motive for getting rid of Tackle was Tackle's attempt to blackmail him over murdering Vernon?"

"Bingo." Jack smiled into Ellery's eyes, and Ellery smiled back.

It was Tuesday evening, and he had just arrived at Jack's for dinner. Jack was filling him in on everything that had happened since Monday night's arrest of James Franklin. Ellery and Jack had barely spoken since James was put into the back of a PICO PD cruiser.

"You okay?" Jack had demanded.

Ellery nodded. It turned out relief left you feeling just as sick and shaky as fear. "I'm okay."

Jack knew Ellery was okay—and that he was the reason Ellery was okay.

"How did you know I might be in trouble?"

"You're *always* in trouble." But Jack sounded rueful not angry. He kissed Ellery once, lingeringly, rested his hand against the side of Ellery's face.

"What am I going to do with you?" he'd murmured.

And that was that. Ellery had driven home to Captain's Seat and spent the rest of the night, Watson curled comfortingly against his back, trying to reassure himself that hadn't been as close a call as it felt.

Tuesday morning Jack had phoned and asked Ellery to dinner, and here Ellery was.

"So James hasn't confessed to anything?"

"Not a thing so far. Not even the attempted abduction of you. He said he repeatedly told you it was too warm and he wasn't feeling very well. He says he just wanted to step outside and chat for a few minutes in the fresh air."

"At gunpoint?"

"That's his story, and he's sticking to it."

"Does he have any explanation for what happened to Vernon?"

"According to James, his father killed Vernon and buried him in the firepit a few yards behind the old Deep Dive."

Ellery shuddered. "What was Douglas's motive supposed to be?"

"Irrational jealousy over Josephine's friendship."

"Then why was Tackle trying to blackmail James?"

Jack said dryly, "Because Tackle knew how distressful it would be for Josephine to discover her husband had killed Vernon over their perfectly innocent friendship."

"He admits Tackle tried to blackmail him, but denies killing him."

"Yep. He says he was more than happy to pay the money to keep Josephine in blissful ignorance. He insists he had nothing to do with Tackle's death."

"What a load of...hogwash."

"Pretty much, yeah."

"Well, did he say how Tackle found out that someone in the Franklin family murdered Vernon?"

"Process of elimination. Rocky always knew it had to be one of the Franklins because Vernon had told him he was going to marry Eudora. Which removed any motive on Eudora's part. Rocky knew *he* hadn't killed Vernon, and he knew Barry and Tony hadn't killed Vernon because of the three of them were together drinking all evening. Tackle might not have realized James was the actual killer. He wouldn't have cared either, so long as someone came up with the money he needed so desperately."

Ellery nodded thoughtfully. "Do you think Josephine had any inkling?"

Jack said neutrally, "Supposedly, Josephine had a month-long breakdown after Vernon went missing. I don't know about you, but that sounds to me like she had some insight into what happened that night."

"It really is pretty tragic all the way around."

"I know." Jack's gaze was grave. "And if you're going to continue digging into other people's tragedies, you're going to have to learn to disengage. You can't take everything to heart."

Ellery sighed, nodded.

"Would you like a glass of wine while I get the food up?"

"I would love a glass of wine." Ellery asked cautiously, "What did you decide to cook?"

"I didn't cook. I ordered from the Seacrest Inn." Jack smiled. "I asked Nan to make us something special."

"*Oh*! What a *great* idea."

Jack snorted. "I'm starting to think you don't like my cooking."

"No way!"

Ellery followed Jack into the immaculate kitchen, leaning against the counter and sipping his wine while Jack carefully unwrapped the foil-topped dishes, plated the stuffed Cornish hens, wild rice, and brussels sprouts. The delicious fragrance of good food well-prepared filled the room. Ellery's stomach growled.

Jack's mouth quirked. "Let me guess. You didn't have time for lunch?"

"I *didn't* have time. Nora and Kingston both called out."

Jack's brows shot up. Ellery said, "I don't think so. I think they're both hungover. They were well on their way from what I could tell last night."

Jack laughed.

"What turned up in that background check on James that made you turn up at the Deep Dive?"

Jack's smile was crooked. "Nothing. Not a damn thing. His record was clean as a whistle."

"Then—"

"Bess Crawford phone to complain about Abel and just happened to mention that she used to be a waitress at the Deep Dive."

"Just happened to mention it? Sure. How many waitresses did they have? There wasn't a single one in the place last night. Reg was doing everything."

"Anyway."

"Sorry. Anyway."

"Bess was also working the night Vernon disappeared. She remembered seeing him go out the back and that James followed him. She also remembered that James always seemed a little intimidated by Vernon, maybe a little scared of him. The fact that she never saw Vernon again after James followed him out, always stuck with her, always made her a little uneasy, but she couldn't believe a kid so young would be capable of murder or that anyone would hush it up."

"That's… Wow."

"Yeah." Jack asked, "So, what have you been up to for the last twenty-four hours? Or do I want to know?"

"Not much. I think my ghost is gone," Ellery remarked. "When I got home last night, there was no light in the window."

Jack made a sound of amusement. "Maybe your ghost had an early call this morning."

"I know it sounds crazy, but I really do think…"

"No, you don't."

After a moment, Ellery said, "Maybe not. But you have to admit it was a funny coincidence."

Jack glanced at him—glanced again. He said, "Who am I to say? I'm not a big believer in ghosts. But there are things out there that can't be easily explained."

Ellery made a face, drained his wineglass. "In other news, I know how those gold coins ended up in the Historical Society's warehouse."

"I've been wondering about that."

"I talked to Vera this morning after she heard James Franklin had been arrested. She admitted hiding the doubloons in the diving bag for safe-keeping. Rocky knew she had them, and after his faculties started to slip, he kept breaking into her house, trying to find them."

"Are you serious?"

"Yep. She thought she'd found the perfect solution, that the warehouse would be safely locked up for decades. And it was. Only the diving suit had already been removed by the time the padlocks went on the doors."

"A comedy of errors," Jack commented. "Only murder isn't funny."

When they carried the hot dishes out to the patio, Ellery discovered, to his horror, that Watson was digging a huge hole in the back corner of the yard.

"*Watson.*"

"That's okay," Jack said easily. "That's his part of the yard."

"His— He has his own part of the yard?"

Jack said a little uncomfortably, "Well…"

Ellery laughed. "You better watch it, Jack. Watson's liable to think you're getting serious about him."

"Ha," Jack said weakly.

Ellery laughed again, turned to the table Jack had set for dinner, and threw Jack a startled look.

"*Wow.* This is so nice." No lie. Candles in small hurricane lanterns. Flowers in a mason jar. Little white lights strung around the patio posts and through the shrubs. He opened his mouth to make some joke—he didn't want to embarrass Jack by making too much of a nice gesture—but Jack looked both pleased and self-conscious.

Jack was doing all of this for Ellery. It was lovely and romantic. Jack *intended* it to be lovely and romantic. He said instead, "I didn't realize it was so pretty out here. We should have eaten out here all summer."

"Shall we sit?" Jack pulled Ellery's chair out.

Ellery sat down. He felt unexpectedly self-conscious, even a little shy. He smiled at Jack.

Jack smiled back and held up the wine bottle. Ellery nodded.

"What should we toast to?"

Jack said quietly, "To life well-lived with those we love."

"That's nice."

Jack filled their glasses. They clinked rims, and the silvery chime floated through the twilight.

The wine was very good. The food was very good. The conversation...

Well, Jack was a little quiet and Ellery was a little nervous. But every time he glanced at Jack, Jack smiled at him, and Ellery felt happy. Happy in a way he couldn't even explain.

Finally, as they were reaching the end of their meals, Jack put his fork down.

"Have you made your mind up about whether you're taking the role in the Happy Halloween reboot?"

"Not yet."

Jack ran a gentle finger over Ellery's knuckles. "Is it that difficult of a decision?"

Ellery lifted a shoulder. "I don't want to do anything that puts strain on our relationship."

Jack's smile faded. His hand stilled. "Do you think our relationship can't take any strain?"

"I don't... I know you really don't like the idea, and that matters to me. I don't want to make you unhappy."

"I don't want to make you unhappy either. If you want the role—"

"I don't know that I want it. I sure as heck don't want it if it ruins things for us."

"Ruins things?" Jack looked taken aback.

Ellery exhaled a long, suddenly shaky breath. "I'm being dramatic. Sorry. I'm just tired. Long day and I didn't sleep much last night."

"Tell me what's worrying you." Jack's voice was so quiet, so gentle, it made Ellery's eyes sting.

"It's silly. I know. I worry about eventually having to let Kingston go or losing the bookshop all together. I worry about losing Captain's Seat. Everything takes so much money."

After a moment, Jack said, "You could sell Skull House."

"No. I can't. I promised Nora she'd be able to use it for the Historical Society. I can't do that to her. Or the island."

"No one on this island expects you to put yourself in financial jeopardy just so the Historical Society has a home."

"I gave my word. I'm not going back on it."

Jack was silent.

"It's okay. I'm going to figure this out."

"Hey, hey," Jack protested. "It *will* be okay. You're not in this alone, you know."

"No, I know." Ellery smiled. "You're the best thing I've got going for me. Which is why no way do I want to do anything to risk that."

"You're not risking anything. If you want that role, I want you to take it. And as for the rest of it… We'll figure something out. Together."

"Yeah."

Jack frowned. He seemed genuinely concerned. "I didn't realize you were this worried. You're always so upbeat. Joking and…"

"I'm mostly *not* worried. I'm probably not worried enough. Most of the time I *do* think everything will work out. But it would be nice to have a little bit of security.

That's all. That's the only reason I'm even considering taking this role."

Jack said abruptly, "Ellery—"

Ellery smiled in inquiry.

"I've...been thinking."

"That sounds serious."

"I *am* serious."

Ellery kept smiling but he was getting a little nervous. Jack's expression was so grave, so intent. If Jack was going to break up with him or deliver bad news, he wouldn't do it with wine and flowers and little twinkly lights painstakingly wound around shrubs and bushes. Wine, flowers, candles seemed to indicate something different. Something Ellery had been determined not to set his heart on.

But as Ellery stared into Jack's dark eyes, the heart in question skipped a hopeful beat. Ellery swallowed.

"I realize eight months isn't that long, but..."

Squeak. Squeak. Squeak.

Watson, who had been contentedly mauling his pale-pink, bug-eyed squeak toy, suddenly hopped up and trotted to the table, compressing the toy maniacally. The toy issued plaintive, high-pitched squeals for help.

Jack and Ellery determinedly ignored the puppy.

"It's long enough to know..."

SqueakEE. SqueakEE. SqueakEE.

Jack cleared his throat. "That is, I didn't think I was ever going to feel like this—feel this much again—feel that someone could matter so much—" He broke off to glare at Watson. Watson grinned around his toy.

SQUEAKeeee. SQUEAKeeee. SQUEAKeeee.

Watson dropped the slimy toy on Jack's foot.

"Oh. My. *God*," Jack groaned. "Every time! Every single freaking time I start this, we get interrupted! This must be my fourth attempt to propose to you!"

"A-are you proposing?"

"Yes! Hell, *yes*, I'm proposing!"

Ellery burst out laughing, bent to snatch up the squeaky toy, and threw it to the very end of Jack's backyard.

Watson directed a look of wounded dignity at him and trotted off—unhurriedly— to retrieve the toy.

Jack sighed, once more reached across the table, taking Ellery's hand. "Ellery, I love you. I love you so much I can't imagine the rest of my life without you. I don't care if you're selling books or making movies or solving mysteries, so long as you're happy. I just want to be with you. I want to share it all. The good times, the bad times, the in-between times—"

"Yes." Ellery interrupted, and he didn't care if Jack saw the tears in his eyes. "*Yes*."

CORPSE AT CAPTAIN'S SEAT

SECRETS AND SCRABBLE BOOK EIGHT

AND THEN THERE WERE... SOME

At long last, the renovations of stately Captain's Seat are mostly complete, and to celebrate, mystery bookseller and sometimes amateur sleuth Ellery Page decides to throw a house-warming party and invite all his New York theater friends to stay for the weekend.

When a freak snowstorm leaves the house party cut off from the village of Pirate's Cove, there's nothing to do but drink, reminisce, and play games. Or so Ellery thinks.

But the only thing more frightening than being forced to play endless hours of charades with *Theatah* People is the possibility of being trapped in a real-life game of Clue.

Preorder now!

AUTHOR'S NOTE

Dear Reader,

Welcome back to Pirate's Cove, where sinister shadows lurk behind every corner of our cute, quaint village. So many secrets. So *many* murders! Such a little police force! Why doesn't someone do something about that? ;-)

These stories are set on fictional Buck Island. The character of Watson is based on my own lunatic adopted pup Spenser (formerly known as Watson).

Thank you as ever to dear, dear Keren. Thank you to Kevin for the endless cups of iced coffee and runs for fast food. Thank you to the Office Elf.

Thank YOU, dear readers. I could not make this voyage without you.

ABOUT THE AUTHOR

Author of over sixty titles of classic Male/Male fiction featuring twisty mystery, kickass adventure, and unapologetic man-on-man romance, JOSH LANYON'S work has been translated into twelve languages. Her FBI thriller *Fair Game* was the first Male/Male title to be published by Harlequin Mondadori, then the largest romance publisher in Italy. *Stranger on the Shore* (Harper Collins Italia) was the first M/M title to be published in print. In 2016 *Fatal Shadows* placed #5 in Japan's annual Boy Love novel list (the first and only title by a foreign author to place on the list). The Adrien English series was awarded the All Time Favorite Couple by the Goodreads M/M Romance Group. In 2019, *Fatal Shadows* became the first LGBTQ mobile game created by *Moments: Choose Your Story.*

She is an Eppie Award winner, a four-time Lambda Literary Award finalist (twice for Gay Mystery), an Edgar nominee, and the first ever recipient of the Goodreads All Time Favorite M/M Author award.

Josh is married and lives in Southern California.

Find other Josh Lanyon titles at www.joshlanyon.com, and follow Josh on Twitter, Facebook, Goodreads, Instagram and Tumblr.

For extras and exclusives, join Josh on Patreon.

ALSO BY JOSH LANYON

NOVELS

The ADRIEN ENGLISH Mysteries
Fatal Shadows • A Dangerous Thing • The Hell You Say
Death of a Pirate King • The Dark Tide
Stranger Things Have Happened • So This is Christmas •

The HOLMES & MORIARITY Mysteries
Somebody Killed His Editor • All She Wrote
The Boy with the Painful Tattoo • In Other Words...Murder

The ALL'S FAIR Series
Fair Game • Fair Play • Fair Chance

The ART OF MURDER Series
The Mermaid Murders •The Monet Murders
The Magician Murders • The Monuments Men Murders
The Movie-Town Murders

BEDKNOBS AND BROOMSTICKS
Mainly by Moonlight • I Buried a Witch
Bell, Book and Scandal

The SECRETS AND SCRABBLE Series
Murder at Pirate's Cove • Secret at Skull House
Mystery at the Masquerade • Scandal at the Salty Dog
Body at Buccaneer's Bay • Lament at Loon Landing
Death at the Deep Dive

OTHER NOVELS

This Rough Magic • The Ghost Wore Yellow Socks
Mexican Heat (with Laura Baumbach) • Strange Fortune
Come Unto These Yellow Sands • Stranger on the Shore
Winter Kill • Jefferson Blythe, Esquire
Murder in Pastel • The Curse of the Blue Scarab
The Ghost Had an Early Check-out
Murder Takes the High Road • Séance on a Summer's Night
Hide and Seek

NOVELLAS

The DANGEROUS GROUND Series
Dangerous Ground • Old Poison • Blood Heat
Dead Run • Kick Start • Blind Side

OTHER NOVELLAS

Cards on the Table • The Dark Farewell • The Dark Horse
The Darkling Thrush • The Dickens with Love
I Spy Something Bloody • I Spy Something Wicked
I Spy Something Christmas • In a Dark Wood
The Parting Glass • Snowball in Hell • Mummy Dearest
Don't Look Back • A Ghost of a Chance
Lovers and Other Strangers • Out of the Blue
A Vintage Affair • Lone Star (in Men Under the Mistletoe)
Green Glass Beads (in Irregulars) • Blood Red Butterfly
Everything I Know • Baby, It's Cold (in Comfort and Joy)
A Case of Christmas • Murder Between the Pages
Slay Ride • Stranger in the House

SHORT STORIES

A Limited Engagement • The French Have a Word for It
In Sunshine or In Shadow • Until We Meet Once More
Icecapade (in His for the Holidays) • Perfect Day
Heart Trouble • Other People's Weddings (Petit Mort)
Slings and Arrows (Petit Mort)
Sort of Stranger Than Fiction (Petit Mort)
Critic's Choice (Petit Mort) • Just Desserts (Petit Mort)
In Plain Sight • Wedding Favors • Wizard's Moon
Fade to Black • Night Watch • Plenty of Fish
Halloween is Murder • The Boy Next Door
Requiem for Mr. Busybody

COLLECTIONS

Short Stories (Vol. 1)
Sweet Spot (the Petit Morts)
Merry Christmas, Darling (Holiday Codas)
Christmas Waltz (Holiday Codas 2)
I Spy...Three Novellas
Dangerous Ground The Complete Series
Dark Horse, White Knight (Two Novellas)
The Adrien English Mysteries Box Set
The Adrien English Mysteries Box Set 2
Male/Male Mystery & Suspense Box Set
Partners in Crime (Three Classic Gay Mystery Novels)
All's Fair Complete Collection
Shadows Left Behind
Fatal Shadows: The Collector's Edition

Printed in the USA
CPSIA information can be obtained
at www.ICGtesting.com
LVHW020814141023
761103LV00009B/791